R.M. CALLAHAN

The Dark Yule

A Pumpkin Spice Tale

First published by Flock Hall Publishing, LLC 2018

Copyright © 2018 by R.M. Callahan

All rights reserved. No part of this publication may be reproduced, stored or transmitted in any form or by any means, electronic, mechanical, photocopying, recording, scanning, or otherwise without written permission from the publisher. It is illegal to copy this book, post it to a website, or distribute it by any other means without permission.

This novel is entirely a work of fiction. The names, characters and incidents portrayed in it are the work of the author's imagination. Any resemblance to actual persons, living or dead, events or localities is entirely coincidental.

R.M. Callahan has no responsibility for the persistence or accuracy of URLs for external or third-party Internet Websites referred to in this publication and does not guarantee that any content on such Websites is, or will remain, accurate or appropriate.

First edition

ISBN: 978-1-7328675-4-3

Editing by Linus Callahan
Proofreading by Theresa Kostelc

*This book was professionally typeset on Reedsy.
Find out more at reedsy.com*

*To my husband,
without whose ideas, support, and profound love
this book would never have been written.*

Contents

Acknowledgement ii
1. Indescribable 1
2. Immemorial 6
3. Antiquated 17
4. Eldritch 28
5. Hideous 41
6. Spectral 60
7. Maddening 82
8. Loathsome 103
9. Unspeakable 117
10. Foetid 136
11. Furtive 150
12. Gibbering 175
13. Mortal 200
14. From the Author 204
15. The Dead Witch 205

About the Author 217
Also by R.M. Callahan 218

Acknowledgement

Many thanks to my husband, from whom I borrowed the idea of "Cats of Cthulhu." Thanks also to Theresa Kostelc, for proofreading; to Saia Ali, for contributing the character Bug; and to my parents, for unfailingly encouraging my writing career from the age of fourteen onwards.

1

Indescribable

It was so dark that I could hardly make out the outline of the night-gaunt. But there it was, perched on the gable directly above the baby's window.

Soon the cloud cover shifted, and the crescent moon shed its dim silver rays across the scene. Now I could see not only the night-gaunt's four bat-like wings, but its small, misshapen head, which was raised to the wind as if to scent my presence—but how could it? The night-gaunt had no nose, nor eyes, nor mouth, nor ears…all things a living being requires, but without which servants of the Great Abyss can do very well.

I stayed where I was, in the shadow of a large fir that bordered my yard. My tail lashed restlessly across the frosty grass. Stilling it by force, I crouched behind some uncut weeds, and peered between their swaying stalks. It occurred to me that, what with the night-gaunt being eyeless and earless and all, it hardly mattered what my tail chose to do.

But there are other senses beyond the five, and it must have availed itself of those. The black head swiveled in my direction. I distinctly heard its hind-claws scrape the roof as it shifted toward me. It leaned over, thrusting its indescribable visage forward, to where I quivered in the shadows.

If I knew anything about night-gaunts, it was about to start gibbering, and that was to be avoided at all costs.

Slowly I stood. My back kept rising long after my legs were extended, until I was braced upon my toes in a perfect arch, my thick fur puffing upright all the way down my spine. I growled at the thing where it waited, so far beyond my reach, and at the same time I calculated where to run should the night-gaunt suddenly take flight. Those tickling paws could seize and carry much heavier beasts than me—I'd seen that for myself.

But I wasn't going to let it hurt my baby.

The night-gaunt crawled forward to the very edge of the cornice, its claws gripping the roof tiles. The *loose* roof tiles, the ones Her Husband had promised time and again to fix, but had never "gotten around to."

A tile broke loose, and the night-gaunt slipped and scrambled for balance, its four membranous wings beating the air. The tile clattered to the deck far below, startling the night-gaunt yet more, and I seized my chance. My growl became a yowl, a vowel-filled incantation against evil I'd learned five lifetimes ago and never forgotten:

"*Iaaaaahhhhhhoooooooorrrrrooooooooooowwyeeeooooooooowwwwy-eeow,*" I shrieked into the night. For good measure I added, in the common language of the dreamlands, "And the same to your mother, too!"

Night-gaunts are not living beings; they don't possess the blind, driving courage required of flesh. The bat-wings continued to beat, and the monster took off. I scrambled to get under the cover of the fir tree. Between its branches I watched, hissing just under my breath, as the unnatural silhouette sailed overhead. Clouds covered the moon again, and the thing was gone.

I listened for Her Husband's swearing, but apparently the house's occupants had slept through the encounter—as they should at this time, when all but the most nocturnal roamed deep in the dreamlands. Emerging slowly from under the fir, I slunk across the yard, waiting until I was a mere body-length from the house to dash forward and dart through the cat-flap in the back door.

With equal caution I proceeded up the stairs, treading lightly upon their stained carpet. I was jumpy as hell and fully expected to see another night-gaunt lurking in some corner, turning its eyeless visage toward me. Instead, the stairs passed without incident. Even before I slipped into the baby's room, I could hear the reassuring sound of his light, feathery breathing.

Up onto the rail of his crib I jumped, and peered into the depths of his cozy nest. He slept on his back, head turned to the left, mouth open; one small, half-closed fist rested by his face, while the other lay buried somewhere under the twisted blanket. I dropped down into a corner of the crib and curled myself around the baby's head. For a moment I fussed with his hair, licking it into good order, and tried not to admit to myself how frightened I'd been.

After all, despite their grim appearance, night-gaunts weren't so bad. Far worse creatures lurked nearby, not only in the shared dreamlands, but in the shadows and vague borders of this material realm. Ghouls roamed the tunnels below our city, feasting on the dead; vengeful spirits spread illness and misfortune by their bleary-eyed stares; and in this part of the world, the Old Ones' delicate influence was often felt, as they manipulated with unseen touches the minds, the hearts, and the very fates of all living beings.

And to this, increasingly, humans were blind. My elders, with fifteen or more lives behind them, recalled when humans could also See That Which Cannot Be Seen. Humans had hung charms in the windows then, to protect their houses—no night-gaunt would have dared approach. They'd worn talismans around their necks, and burned big bonfires at the proper time of year, and left food offerings and sacrifices deep in the woods. They'd recited fairy tales and fables to their children, with all the good gory bits intact, because knowing what to do when the Old Woman of the Forest approached wasn't a matter of entertainment, but of survival.

Yet as the humans had become more clever, they'd grown less wise. A terrible creeping blindness had taken them: they could not see what they did not believe in. But what they did not believe in still existed, and was in fact growing more powerful—more free and unconstrained by the day. Perhaps that was why a night-gaunt, which should never have drifted outside the dreamlands, had been perched above my baby's window. Whether it had come for good or ill, it didn't belong here, and that was a problem.

I considered this as I groomed my baby's hair. When he at last stirred I leapt back out of the crib, balancing myself upon the rail. Stretching high, I sank two claws into the wall paper and drew them down and across, scratching an old sign of protection just above my baby's head. Surely I'd be yelled at for it the next day, since Her Husband never could tell the difference between a proper Mark and recreational clawing, but given what I'd just witnessed, I wasn't about to take a chance.

If the humans wouldn't protect their own, then we cats would just have to do it for them.

2

Immemorial

I curled myself around my baby's cold feet, and purred myself into the dreamlands.

The soft mattress under my claws hardened to stone. Black shadows on the wall, cast by the trees outside, took on form and dimension of their own. Their roots crawled across the carpet, piercing through to earth; their sprouting branches lifted the roof away and exposed the distant stars.

I was no longer in my baby's room, but crouched upon a high, craggy boulder in the middle of a dark pine forest. From this vantage point I surveyed the night scene as best as I could, ears twisting to catch any sound. There were none, not even the random squawk of a bird or the chirp of a cricket. This forest wasn't designed to feel natural; in fact, it wasn't designed at all. It was merely a collective realm of archetypes, a vast common space tread into being by the movement of millions of minds.

There was a mist gathering rapidly between the trees—a bad sign. Not ten body-lengths from me, a blurred shadow drifted past. It was a big shadow, approximately human-sized and human-shaped, though that didn't mean much in these shared realms. It wasn't common, but I'd encountered sleepers from other stars before.

This sleeper was clearly unconscious, just an unawakened figure rambling aimlessly through self-created dreams. It either didn't see the fog billowing before it, or didn't know what that meant. If it had been someone I recognized, I might have tried to steer the dreamer in another direction, or to startle them awake; but just as they were a mere shadow of movement to me, so was I hardly visible to them. There was little to nothing I could do.

I leaped down from the boulder, taking care to skirt the edge of the seething, roiling mist. A pair of yellow eyes within it watched me go round, but made no effort to seize me. Dream hags don't feed upon cats. We're too conscious, even when sleeping, to make good prey. But the average human, who stumbles through the shallowest dreamlands half-aware and forgetful, is an ideal victim. Given the chance, they'll pursue especially tasty souls right into the material realms. I'd once chased a particularly persistent one off of Morwen's chest.

These surface-level dreamlands were rarely fatal, but that didn't mean they weren't dangerous. More than hags lurked here. Ghosts returned to try, usually in vain, to speak to lost loved ones, and touchy spirits tormented those mortals who'd crossed them. Sometimes you even encountered a god strolling through woods like these, imposing carefully-designed dreams upon weaker, more malleable minds.

In short, it was no place to linger, and I had no intention of doing so. I wanted to descend to deeper and more interesting realms. Through the woods I continued apace, ignoring the unpleasant prickling of the dried pine needle carpet.

The last wisps of mist cleared, the trees grew sparser

and shorter amidst scattered stones, and then there was my doorway: a sheer flint cliff, its deadly drop half-disguised by the tips of trees growing far below. One tree, a king of pines, reared its head far above the rest, stretching nearly to the top of the cliff. Its battle-scarred, needle-less top quivered in the breeze not a tail-length from me.

This was a dreamlands doorway popular only with cats; I'm sure you can understand why. It was an easy enough jump, though, so long as you possessed claws. I bundled my hind legs beneath me and launched myself at the bare top of the pine. My claws sank satisfyingly into the old, soft wood, so that while the branches swayed dangerously beneath my bulk, I was as firmly latched to the bark as a tick. I would need to grip hard—the worst was yet to come.

In the distance, I heard a faint scream. The dream hag had seized her prey, and was feasting upon his helplessness and fear. I hoped he awakened soon.

With care I edged my way down the enormous trunk. At first the climb grew easier, for the further I went, the less vertical the great tree became. That is to say, the tree itself didn't move, but my perspective gently shifted around it, so that as I crawled down the trunk, it appeared to become more and more horizontal—like a log bridge rather than a tree. In mere moments I was sauntering along its length, my plumed tail waving in the whistling breeze. It was easy so long as I didn't look at the ground, which was now an earthy wall to my right. On my left stretched the yawning gray sky. Do more than glance to either side, and you were likely to become totally disoriented, and fall. Fall to where? Who could say?

Next came a tangle of roots, long stripped of their finer filaments by the rubbing of countless furred backs. I squeezed myself between them. Once again my perspective slowly rotated, as if the world were a framed picture being turned right way up. In short order I was, once again, climbing a tree—but I was only a short ways off the ground, and in a different place altogether, far from the grim communal forest.

The tree I clutched was no longer the scarred giant of the forest, but a graceful, white-barked birch. From this I leapt down and, twisting over my own back, commenced licking my fur into place. This gesture offered me the chance both to observe, and to be observed. I was curious who was here tonight.

There was nothing shared about this dreamland: it was purely a place of cats. I doubted it had been designed by felines, though, for it appeared to have once been a glorious human city. It was always sunset in this dreamland. Golden light lingered along the arched bridges that spanned the overgrown canals, and laid gorgeous blue shadows below crumbling walls. Shattered red roof tiles were half-hidden on the grassy cobbles, and broad, leafy trees thrust their roots up between the stones. There were no people anywhere, but there were plenty of mice, and rats, and voles, and songbirds, and every other kind of vermin that thrived in ruins. These were only figments of dream, naturally, but they still squeaked when you caught them, and that was what mattered.

Plenty of black shadows slunk by, and long tails dangled from low-hanging branches, but they belonged to cats only semi-visible to me. Most of us do not care to socialize with strangers, even in the dreamlands.

At last I spotted Libby, who lived two blocks down from me, and remained one of the few outdoor-roaming cats on our side of town. Libby was a Devon Rex, which is just about the silliest-looking kind of cat there is, if you ask me, but he was proud of his British ancestry and prominent, bat-like ears. He was grooming himself in his usual graceless fashion, with his back leg sticking straight out over his head. Probably he was demonstrating that he was an intact Tom, as if his powerful musk alone wasn't enough of a hint.

Following a long stretch and a yawn, I strolled over. He ignored me at first, continuing to rasp his tongue along the fine, slightly wavy fur of his stomach. I was getting a good look at his hairy balls, but they had no effect upon me: I'd been fixed at six months and was above all that nonsense. My baby was the only kit I'd ever raise.

I sat beside him, rubbed my shoulder against his, and laid a friendly tongue over his ear, right at the back where it's hard to reach. He purred and leaned into me, tucking his leg back where it belonged.

Having established the terms of our encounter, I could now speak. "Hey, Libby. Have you seen anything unusual in the neighborhood?"

Though I'd ceased grooming him, Libby's eyes remained half-closed, and his purr trilled on. "The king's here tonight," he remarked sleepily.

"Oh." I searched for something to say. "Is he a panther again?"

Libby dipped his head in assent, still purring slightly. My tail twitched, and my claws extended to scrape the stones. I didn't think much of a king who took so flashy a dream form, but there was no point in sharing that with Libby. As a fixed female who matched King Jack pound for pound, I could afford to be nearly nasty. As a small, unneutered male in the King's territory, Libby couldn't afford any opinion at all.

Instead, I clarified. "I meant in the *physical* neighborhood."

Libby's eyes opened to green slits. "Hmm. Not really. We do have some new guests at the B&B."

"Oh?"

"They're staying through Christmas they said. I think they're photographers. They have a lot of those, what-d'you-call-them, cameras, and they're always off on long walks through the town."

"Hmm." I considered this. "It doesn't sound suspicious."

At last Libby focused upon me. "What're you up to, Spice?" he asked, in tones of deep disapproval.

"Nothing important," I said. And then, casually—and keeping my tail carefully still—I added, "I chased a night-gaunt off our roof tonight. Thought you might have seen one, too."

Libby's pupils exploded open, shrinking the green iris down to an iridescent ring. "A night-gaunt? In the material realm? At my house?!"

"At *my* house," I corrected, lifting my paw to my mouth and giving it a cool little lick. "On the baby's window. But I frightened it away. I know a good incantation, if you think you'll need it."

Libby gulped audibly. I could feel his tail lashing against my hindquarters. "What's a night-gaunt doing outside the dreamlands?"

"No idea." I continued to give my paw a delicate bath, and tried not to purr with satisfaction at his reaction.

"I agree," said someone behind me. "What's a night-gaunt doing outside the dreamlands?" A battered-looking white cat slunk around to face me, her tail tracing a long, delicate line along my side.

It was Dorothy, better known as Dot, from three blocks down and two blocks over. She had a face as crooked as a street-fighting feral's, but in her case, appearances were misleading. In fact, her human was quite wealthy and pampered Dot, being particularly generous on the subject of sardines. Even now the rich, heavenly whiff of canned fish lingered in Dot's fur.

"I'm sure I don't care," I told her in a sniffy way, not wanting to admit how frightened I'd been. "But I put up a Mark, just in case."

"I thought Her Husband was going to declaw you if you scratched any more of the wallpaper?"

"Morwen won't let him," I said firmly.

"It's not so bad, being declawed," another cat chimed in. A long, spotted tail dangled from a nearby branch, though its owner remained hidden by leaves. This was Cinnamon, a Savannah cat hardly older than a kitten, and the newest addition to our neighborhood. "You get used to it."

I refrained from pointing out that, as a declawed cat, she could hardly hope to climb a tree outside the dreamlands. "Have you seen a night-gaunt?" I asked her point-blank.

"Not in this lifetime," she replied.

I personally found Cinnamon profoundly irritating. It was bad enough that the Savannah cat rivaled me in size. Equally offensive was her name, which was far too close to my own. But the fact that Cinnamon was my elder by several lives *really* got under my tail. It didn't help that she seemed none too bright in this lifetime, though I was never quite sure whether she was genuinely obtuse, or merely ignorant.

"Then you're no help," I snapped at her, and stalked, stiff-legged, down the street, in the direction of the glorious setting sun.

I ignored the half-seen shadows of strange cats, and the tempting rustling sounds in piles of fallen autumn leaves, whose delightful crunch co-existed with the fresh green foliage overhead. The dreamlands are full of such pleasant contradictions.

Personally I preferred my own proprietary patch of trees, which represented the last remnants of timber belonging to the old, old house. I thought of crouching under that big fir not long ago, and of watching the silhouette of the night-gaunt flap across the waning moon.

What if it had returned in my spiritual absence? Could it even now be knocking against the window of my baby's room, while he and I slept on, oblivious?

I felt my dream-self slipping back into wakefulness, and resisted the subtle urge to open my eyes. I wanted time to think about all this, and the material world was not always conducive to deep consideration. In particular, I wanted to be both alone, and somewhere up high—all cats know elevation is necessary to proper cogitation.

I approached a likely-looking tree. Bunching my hind legs beneath me, I prepared to launch myself at the nearest low-hanging branch—and stopped. An enormous black paw was just visible between in the gap between the leaves, and a second glance showed me the gleam of a massive, liquid eye within the beech's dappled shadows.

"Your Highness," I said. "My apologies."

"No apology required, Pumpkin Spice," said the panther, with an undertone that might have been either a growl, or a purr. "I hear you bear troubling news."

How had he known? Had he tapped into mysterious kingly powers to learn the content of my conversation? Or had he merely eavesdropped? It was impossible to say. Besides, I was more miffed about him using my full name, though perhaps that wasn't strictly fair. Likely the king simply didn't recall that I preferred "Spice." I was a fixed female on the edge of his territory and, as such, hardly deserved his consideration.

"I saw a night-gaunt," I told him, craning my head back to better observe the panther above me. Deliberately or not, the king remained nearly invisible amidst the thick foliage. "In the material world," I clarified, after a second's pause produced no response.

"Is that all?" the king wanted to know.

Isn't that enough? I wanted to ask. "It seems unusual," I demurred instead.

"What did it do?"

"I tried an incantation on it, and it flew away." Stated baldly, my adventure appeared less than impressive.

"Just one night-gaunt?" the king asked.

"Just the one."

The panther paused. I was becoming tired of sitting with my head practically laid against my back, but it's hard to look away from a cat that big. It's not very wise, either.

"Well, it is Kingsport," he said at last. "Visitors aren't uncommon, are they? I wouldn't worry about it. Go about your business."

I blinked at the king respectfully, and trotted lightly away. I managed to make it around a corner before my tail lashed and my ears flattened against my head.

Well, it is Kingsport! And what did Jack know? He'd only been king two years, after that highly-questionable defeat of the far-more-beloved Big Red, and he'd only been in Kingsport a year before that. I'd been born and raised in Kingsport, and I knew with certainty that this was at least my second life in the area. I had vague memories that stretched back even further, to white-sailed ships and muddy lanes, so it was possible I'd accumulated three or even four lifetimes in this location. Such repetition was not unheard of, though it was unusual.

This time, I managed to find an unoccupied tree, and leapt aggressively upon a wide, comfortable branch. Violently sharpening my claws on the soft bark improved my mood, and as I scratched, I came to two conclusions.

First, it was possible that I'd seen a night-gaunt, and no one else had, because the night-gaunt had been drawn to our house in particular. Granted, it had been an age since Morwen had worked any magic, and she hadn't been much good to start. Still, it might be worth sniffing around the house, to see if she'd dabbled in the occult again. To be perfectly honest, I rather hoped she had. I'd enjoyed being a familiar.

Second, the person to speak with wasn't King Jack, but Tilly. The immemorial Tilly was an old crone of a cat who'd stubbornly refused to die—every neighborhood had one. She'd know if a night-gaunt was unusual (even for Kingsport), or if my concerns were misplaced. If Tilly didn't see any cause for alarm, and if Morwen hadn't been getting up to magical shenanigans, I'd just have to let the whole matter drop.

Like most ancient cats, Tilly spent three-quarters of her life in the dreamlands, with no more than an occasional, drowsy appearance in the material realm for food or a piss. She was almost certainly in the dreamlands now. I leapt down from the tree, ready to search for her…

…and awoke with a shriek as something seized the back of my neck. Choking, I fought the strong grip. I was rising into the air…I could see the shadow of the night-gaunt stretched below me…

Then I saw what was *actually* below me: my sleeping baby.

The edge of the crib. And then the floor, as I was flung violently down. With a half-twist I landed on my feet and instantly jetted out the door, squeezing past Morwen's slippered foot as she stomped into the room.

Her Husband was yelling, probably at me, but I never understood anything he said—his speech was just noises in the air, with none of that subtle spiritual comprehension that exists between true companions. I picked up much more of the meaning behind Morwen's exasperated sounds. *Damn it, don't throw the cat! Baby is fine...cats don't suffocate infants...a myth.* Then my baby awoke with his characteristic roar, and both human parents were occupied.

In a quiet corner of the kitchen I licked my fur back into place, vigorously stripping the smell of Her Husband's hand from my neck. Then I squeezed through the back door's slightly-too-small cat flap, almost losing my footing on the deck's half-melted morning frost.

It was true that Tilly's soul was almost certainly in the dreamlands, even now. However, it was also true that a great dream traveler like herself could be anyplace, whereas I knew exactly where to find her physical body. As for the humans, I hoped they noticed I'd left in a huff. It would serve them right.

3

Antiquated

Despite my ridiculously early rising, getting to Tilly's house would be no easy task. This was partially due to traffic on the large road, Walnut Street, that divided my territory from hers. Walnut Street was the road by which King Jack and the previous monarch, Big Red, had held their fateful duel. Jack had rolled Big Red onto the street, and a large truck struck his ginger opponent, leaving Jack the somewhat doubtful victor.

I hadn't been there in person, but like all the neighborhood cats, I'd known at once that our king was dead. Such knowledge strikes one as a sudden blast of cold air; for just a moment, your mind freezes with cold clarity, and you see the world through ice. Since that day I'd taken extra care on Walnut Street.

Mostly, however, the difficulty lay in the half-wild dogs that dwelt on the corner of Walnut and Jefferson. They called themselves the Bastard Pack. We called them pretentious jerks. There was a Mastiff, a Dane, and two Pit Bulls, but their leader was a standard poodle called Mo, and he was by far the meanest of the lot. Poodles usually are.

Dogs are rarely a problem to us free-roaming cats—so long as we have claws, and the neighborhood boasts plenty of trees, fences, and low-hanging roofs—but the owner of the Bastard Pack was a beer-swilling low-life who couldn't be bothered with something like basic fence repair. Thus his "fence" was more of a faint wooden suggestion, barely able to stand up to a stiff breeze, let alone five large, aggressive, cat-hunting dogs. If I wanted to survive a visit to Tilly's, I'd either have to take care they didn't scent me, or stay high enough that it wouldn't matter.

I wove my way through the series of backyards and bare hedges that would lead me to Walnut Street. The pink light of the sunrise was reflected by the clouds, which hung low and luminous with unshed snow. The whole morning enjoyed a pleasant sort of glow, a hushed sense of expectation. It was also cold as hell, and my breath puffed whitely before me as I slunk through a neighbor's garden. In warmer weather I'd have left little footprints in in the soft soil, telling tales of my passing, but in this season the ground was frozen hard.

It was a time to hunker down and enjoy the pleasures of the indoors: crackling flames in the house's old fireplace, with its cracked bricks and persistent draft; a soft blanket to knead under my tired, cold paws; a warm lap in which to snuggle and snooze. Morwen's growing belly, heavy with her second kit, didn't leave much room for said snuggling, but I still felt obligated to try. It was good to purr sweet little nothings to the unborn within, so that it might recognize my voice when it emerged. Gods, though, human birthings did take forever! Had I been unfixed, I could've borne three entire litters in the time it took Morwen to form a single child.

Busy with such contemplations, I hardly noticed where I was, until the fence I was walking ended abruptly. My front paw was actually dangling in mid-air before I could stop; I had to execute an awkward little pretend-grooming session, licking the paw's side and smoothing it over my head—just in case any other cat had been watching.

As I performed the pantomime, I took a good look at Walnut Street. To my disappointment the traffic was as heavy as ever. There was hardly any pause in the stream of vehicles, let alone a gap lengthy enough for a cat to dash across. Speed was not my greatest asset; better to leave the mad sprints to smaller, whippier cats.

That left the crosswalk at the corner, directly opposite the home of the Bastard Pack. I couldn't hear the dogs, but I could smell their lingering reek all the way down the street, so it was difficult to say whether or not they occupied the yard this morning. I debated the possibility that they were eating breakfast. Morning seemed a rational time to feed big, hungry beasts, but their degenerate owner hardly seemed the type to stick to a schedule.

Perched on the narrow fence, watching the cars speed by, I found myself fixated upon the idea of breakfast. Delicious breakfast…moist and savory…what was it, exactly, that I was craving? I sniffed the frigid air and corrected myself. Not craving: smelling. What was it that I smelled?

I dropped off the fence and wandered down the sidewalk, a little nearer to the teasing odor. It seemed to emerge from the storm drain in the gutter. I halted, disappointed. I knew better than to try and go down there. Kingsport lost kittens every year to the sewers.

Yet the aroma intrigued me. It smelled somewhat like tuna,

and yet, not at all like tuna. It was definitely fish, and raw at that. Were there actual fish swimming in the sewers now? Perhaps some koi abandoned by a careless human, grown to enormous size? I wondered what it would take to locate a safe entrance to the sewers, and organize a little hunting party. Dot would be interested, I was sure—for such a well-fed and pampered cat, she was an inveterate and unsympathetic hunter, and the terror of the neighborhood songbirds.

With care I crept to the edge of the sidewalk, hoping for a better whiff. My ears flattened as a car sped by, too close for comfort. I'd have to sniff quick. As soon as the next car tore past, I dropped my head over the side, and inhaled deeply.

A scaly, fishy, horribly *slimy* paw closed over my head, crushing my face. It was dragging me down the hole!

I shrieked and sank my claws into the pungent, disgustingly spongy flesh, as deeply as they could possibly go. I'd hoped to touch bone, but then again, I wasn't entirely sure there were any. At the same time I launched myself upwards with a powerful thrust of my hind legs, fighting that awful downward pressure.

The paw, or hand, or whatever it was, spasmed under my claws, loosening its grip for a critical second just as I made my leap. I ended up somersaulting forward, to land ungracefully upon my back in the middle of the street. With a twist and a roll I snaked out of the creature's slackened grasp, at the same time releasing my own death grip. Now free, I sprang upright onto my toes, spitting and hissing into the face of my assailant.

But all I could see was the storm drain's low opening, gaping blackly. There was no sign of my attacker.

A car horn honked madly, and I remembered where I was: in the road! I leapt into the air, twisted mid-jump, and dashed pell-mell away from the sewer. This took me directly into oncoming traffic, but whatever spirits or guardians look after me were in good form that day. Three cars slammed on their brakes, and I heard more horns behind me, but in two breathless, terrifying seconds I had gained the opposite sidewalk and was hurtling top-speed toward Tilly's house.

From here it was all old, narrow, quiet neighborhood roads, with nothing to dodge but an occasional trundling car bumping over the cracked asphalt—and those were easily avoided by staying high. I did pause to wash the fish smell from my head, a nasty task that took longer than I'd expected.

At last I dropped off an old stone wall and into the handkerchief-sized square of greenery that was Tilly's "backyard." It was primarily occupied by an out-of-place koi pond, whose surface gleamed with translucent ice. On a flat rock beside the pond was a ratty pink blanket, and on this blanket, posed with paws outstretched like a particularly small, mangy, and grumpy Sphinx, was Tilly.

I usually encountered Tilly in the dreamlands. There, whether she appeared in the sunset city or the cat-thronged streets of Ulthar, she was young and black-furred, with a star of white upon her chest, and eyes as green as a frog. I'd come to understand that this was Tilly clinging to the appearance of a previous, and far more exciting, incarnation.

In this lifetime she was only a rather dull gray tabby, and her pupils had grown increasingly milky with age. In fact, though she opened her eyes at my approach, I wasn't entirely sure she could see me at all. But then, did an elder cat like Tilly really require physical senses?

She didn't bother to turn and face me; instead, a single ear cocked in my direction. "Pumpkin Spice," she muttered. "What do you want?"

Though she wasn't looking at me, I blinked twice and settled into a crouch before responding, "I could use some advice, Elder." You see? I could be respectful at times, if the other party was deserving.

Tilly's eyes lazily closed again. She yawned, showing the brown remnants of teeth, and a goodly dose of gum disease. "Meet me in the dreamlands," she commanded, and dropped her head upon her chest, preparing to doze her way into alternate realms.

I actually wasn't very good at moving in and out of the dreamlands on cue—I required darkness and genuine exhaustion to make the transition. Libby, by contrast, could pass between worlds with a blink and a sneeze. But how could I possibly admit that? "Ah, Tilly…" I began, stalling for time. An excuse manifested abruptly, and I seized it. "I want to ask you about the night-gaunts," I told her. "And I've heard that if you whisper their name too much in the dream realms, they'll return to haunt your sleep."

Tilly's eyes snapped open. "True," she said. "Better safe than sorry." And just when I thought I'd gotten away with it, she added, "And besides, I'd forgotten how clumsy your dream-entries are."

This I ignored. "I found a night-gaunt on my roof," I explained. "Last night."

"Interesting," Tilly mumbled, sounding profoundly bored. She didn't say anything for another few moments. I was beginning to think she'd dozed off again, and left for the dreamlands without me, when she asked, "What about your human? What's-her-nose, the little wannabe witch? Has she been at it again?"

"Morwen?" I said. "I don't think so. I'm certain I would've noticed her workings." In truth, I wasn't certain at all, because Tilly wasn't totally wrong—very little of Morwen's magic had *actually* worked. She'd still been at the my-magic-books-have-colorful-covers-and-come-from-the-mall-bookstore phase when she'd met Her Husband and ceased her practice. For all I knew, she might have been casting her "spells" with abandon, and I'd never have noticed a thing.

Still, I felt compelled to defend my "wannabe" witch's honor. "She'll pick it up again, after this next kit's born," I told Tilly, with far more hope than conviction.

Tilly sneezed. "I hope so," she said, quite unexpectedly. "We could use any half-decent witch. This town is going to hell in a handbasket because the damn humans can't see past their whiskers. If they had whiskers. You know what I mean." Once again, her ear twitched in my direction, though her clouded eyes still stared into the distance. "And this generation of cats isn't much better. Your mother was good at Seeing That Which Cannot Be Seen. I thought you'd inherited her gift. But here you are, babbling about night-gaunts, which ought to be the least of your worries."

I started to reply, to question—and stopped. Sitting upright, paws together, I rotated my tufted ears, and stared over Tilly's back at the iced-over pond. Eyes unfocused, I searched for That Which Cannot Be Seen.

Tantalizing fishy shadows slid beneath the ice. These I tried to ignore…until I realized that their numbers had abruptly tripled. For an eyeblink, dozens of black shapes writhed beneath the surface of the water, in a place where I knew only a few ferociously tough carp survived.

Next I turned my attention to the withered, stunted corpse

of a long-dead bonsai on the other side of the pond. I concentrated my whole being upon the bare brown branches, until I dropped into a deeper state of consciousness, where thought merely babbled in the background, and primal, unceasing awareness took hold.

Time slowed. My eyes jerked, involuntarily, to the left. The bonsai vanished. It reappeared a second later, blurring itself slowly back into position. However, its shadow was at a different angle, one that did not correspond to the sun's position.

I swore, and blinked repeatedly, until things looked mostly normal again. The bonsai's shadow, however, was still not at quite the right degree.

Tilly emitted a rusty-sounding purr. "You see," she said. "I'm not surprised you saw *one* night-gaunt. I'm surprised you haven't seen a dozen. Not to mention a lot of other, much worse beasties besides."

The fur was rising on my spine, a stiff, prickly manifestation of fear. "What's happening?" I demanded. "What is this… dislocation?"

"I don't know," said Tilly. Damn her, she didn't sound concerned at all. "Interesting, isn't it?"

A past-life memory tickled the back of my synapses. "Time often gets slippery around the solstice," I suggested. It seemed true, but I could also sense that I hadn't quite grasped the memory correctly.

"Fair enough," said Tilly, shutting one eye. "But this is more than a bit. And it's more than time."

"It's space as well," I agreed.

"In the old days, I wouldn't have worried," said Tilly. "Not this close to Yule. The humans would've burned bonfires and beaten the bounds of the town. Their prayers and songs would have marked this place as theirs, as surely as a tomcat's spray, and the blood of the sacrifices would've appeased every spirit within a day's travel."

Tilly's memories went back further than mine—I could not recall a time of animal sacrifices. "Or," I suggested, "the church bells would've rung on Christmas morn."

"Or that," Tilly agreed. "And the world would've slipped back into its rightful track, without any fuss."

"But not now," I said. It was half a question.

"Not now," said Tilly flatly. "Reality has been sadly neglected. Frankly, I'm surprised it's held up this long."

A sudden scratching sound came from the back wall, and I hissed. "Who's there?" I demanded, my back arching.

Libby poked his ridiculous, bat-eared head over the top of the antiquated bricks. "It's me! I've been looking for you everywhere!"

"Everywhere?" I questioned, slowly resuming my seat.

"Well, at your house," Libby admitted, pulling himself over the wall and jumping into the yard. "Here was next. But anyway! Pumpkin Spice!"

"Present," I affirmed, closing my eyes and purring.

"I saw a night-gaunt! No, I saw two!"

My eyes snapped fully open, and my pupils dilated, so that with dazzling clarity I could perceive every whisker and hair upon Libby's bony muzzle. "Where? When?" I demanded.

"On my roof! MY roof!" Libby seemed indignant about this, as if night-gaunts belonged solely on other people's roofs. "I tried to get Mark to see them when he was getting in his car, but they just flew off before he could turn around."

"It wouldn't have done any good," Tilly murmured. "So few

humans these days can See That Which Cannot Be Seen."

"Well, you needn't tell me that," Libby huffed. "I just got smacked silly for clawing his pants. Why do humans make such a fuss about a few tiny holes?"

"Do you think they're attracted to what's happening to the town?" I asked Tilly.

Tilly frowned and, for the first time, turned her ghostly, unseeing eyes upon me. "Of course," she said. "And as I said, I'm surprised we're not downright swarmed with creatures from all hundred and eight realms. They're bound to be attracted to this mess."

"What's going on? What's happening to the town?" Libby demanded.

Tilly ignored him. "But, then again…night-gaunts. Hmm. It *is* odd."

"What is?" I pressed.

"Oh. Well, I'm sure they're drawn to all this, but…"

"But?" I prompted her.

"But generally they just sort of *hover* near the edges, you know, drifting between our world and the dreamlands. To be pulled this far into the material realm, they've usually got to be summoned." Her tail twisted and thrashed in thought. "I suppose it could have something to do with the ghouls."

"The ghouls?" I asked.

"Ghouls and night-gaunts have an ancient alliance," Tilly explained. "It's mostly in the dreamlands, but…"

"It's not as though Kingsport doesn't have an *infestation* of ghouls," said Libby, with a fastidious shudder. He licked his paw and ran it over his ear as if to wash away the very thought. "There are more of those canine bastards every year."

"Yes, and they're on the move," said Tilly. "I've heard them scampering about their tunnels, during all hours of daylight, no less."

Tunnels! I'd nearly forgotten to tell Tilly of the creature I'd encountered—a creature whose presence now took on ghastly implications. "Speaking of tunnels and creatures and so forth," I began, "something in the gutters tried to *eat* me this morning."

"So it begins," said Tilly, and yawned. When I tried to speak again, she made a warning noise deep in her throat. I stopped.

"I'm tired," she told Libby and me. "This lifetime won't last past Christmas, not if I'm lucky, and I'd like to end it in peace. So whatever is happening now, it's on you young things. My advice is to take a look at the ghouls. Get one to talk to you."

"Uh, how?" Libby asked, tilting his head. "Why would *any* ghoul talk to a cat?"

Tilly's eyes were closed, and her chin was dropping slowly, jerkily, toward her chest. My senses, sharpened by the recent vision, could see her figure dim as her soul slipped away into the dreamlands, where she was once again young, and beautiful, and powerful.

4

Eldritch

We used the crosswalk at the corner of Walnut St. this time, but only after exploratory sniffs confirmed that the Bastard Pack had already jumped their sorry excuse for a fence, and were roaming free elsewhere.

Well, all except for one.

"I smell the fish," said Libby. We were crouched on the sidewalk, a safe distance from where I'd nearly been pulled down into the sewer. "And dog." He paused. "And blood."

"Are you sure?" I asked. My own nose isn't as good as Libby's.

"It's faint but it's there," he said. "What do you think? Did one of the Bastard Pack get too close?"

"If so, it'd have to be one of the Pits," I said. "I don't think anything bigger could fit down there."

"And you have no idea what it was?" Libby asked for what must have been the fifth time.

"I *said* no. I've never seen a...a fishy, person, *thing* in the sewers before. Have you?"

Libby shuddered. "This is putting me right off fish," he

muttered, backing away from that ominous opening in the gutter. "I hope Mark and Clarence bought the lamb flavor last night. I'll have to turn my nose up at anything else and hope they take the hint."

"Morwen always gets whatever's cheapest at the store."

"No wonder you hunt so much," Libby sympathized, swiping past me with a friendly shoulder-rub.

We leapt atop the fence and meandered onward, single-file. The day was warming beautifully. It was the perfect time for a lengthy nap in a sunny spot on the floor, and I knew without asking that was likely Libby's plan as well as my own.

Still, Libby paused when it came time for us to part ways, at a quiet corner not far from my house. "I'm not sure I want to go home," he confessed, easing his butt down upon the narrow fence and squinting at the bright winter sky. "*Two* night-gaunts at my house, Spice. That's twice as many as at yours."

"Well, you can't come home with me," I reminded him. "At least, not if Her Husband is home today. He won't tolerate more than one cat. "

"And he yells so *loudly.*" Libby flicked his ear in memory. "I suppose I'd better go back. What would Mark and Clarence do if one of those things got *inside*? Even if they could see it, they'd be helpless as kittens."

"You've got to be there to warn them," I affirmed.

"Hah! Fat lot of good it does. You should see the nasty creatures that get into our house sometimes. The guests bring them, I think. There was this little black thing that walked on two legs but was the size of a rat—it came in one of the guest's suitcases and lived in the hall shadows for *weeks.* I tried to swipe the damn thing every time I saw it, but my paw just passed through." Libby held up said paw, contemplated it, and nibbled at an overlong claw.

"Did it bite?" I asked.

"Not me," said Libby, after spitting out a fragment of nail. "But it went after the guests once or twice. One of them accused Mark and Clarence of having bed-bugs, even though the bites were all wrong. Such a kerfuffle! And of course, for at least a month it was, 'Stop *yowling*, Libby, there's *nothing* there!'"

"Oh, of course."

Libby inspected his paw, decided it passed muster, and eased into a long, yawning stretch. The bright sun doubtless made him languid, as it did me; night-gaunts and time-slips and even shadow-rats all suddenly seemed capable of waiting. "At least," Libby added, "your Morwen knows a *bit* about magic."

"Hmm. It's nothing to count on," I admitted. This was a good reminder, though: I'd meant to check up on possible occult activity in our home. I had better do it at once. "Well, see you later, Libby."

"I'll dream of you," he said, rather formally, and jumped down, slinking through a small gap in the next door neighbor's fence.

By the time I'd reached my own house I could barely keep my eyes open, but I'd made a promise to myself, and it's bad habit to break those—it wreaks havoc not only on one's psyche, but also on one's magic. How can you expect the universe to obey your commands, if even *you* ignore them? So I slipped through the cat door and went straight to the stairs.

I heard the television blaring in the living room as I passed, and easily smelled the patchouli reek of the newest in a long line of babysitters. My baby was shrieking along with whatever was playing on the devil-box so I knew he was well, although if a kitten had made noises like that I would have smacked him. Humans are different, though—so much depends on the quality and quantity of their squawking language. Silence does not come naturally to them.

The carpeted stairs took me to the bedrooms. A second flight of bare wooden stairs brought me to the attic. The door was closed, but the handle was a simple lever. I stood up on my back legs and pawed at it, and the door fell open with a welcoming click. I was lucky it hadn't been locked. Perhaps Morwen *had* been up here after all.

As soon as I stepped inside, however, I knew I'd been wrong. Nobody had used this little room for quite some time. There was a thick coating of dust on the worn wooden floorboards, and in the air it was heavy enough to make me sneeze once—twice—three times. Stacks of cardboard boxes leaned precariously in random locations, and my baby's bassinet was standing on end against the dirty window. What had once been Morwen's special place had been given over to storage.

Nonetheless, it paid to be sure. When my sneezing fit had finished, I stepped forward to inspect the barely-visible remnants of the chalk circle. No sign of renewal. I then negotiated my way around several moldering boxes, to the writing desk that still held Morwen's small magical library. It was an antique, that desk, one that Morwen had brought home in great excitement—I'd gathered she'd considered herself lucky to find such a beautiful old specimen. Luckier than she knew, perhaps, because from my perspective it was easy to spot the eldritch symbols carved into its underside. Even now, when I looked to See That Which Cannot Be Seen, a faint aura of magic clung to the age-polished wood, like the lingering aroma of rare incense. Kingsport was quite an old settlement, after all, and its residents had carried on certain rites and rituals for longer than many other towns, even in this tradition-loving area. It was really not so surprising that the property of one practitioner should pass to the hands of another—and, perhaps, it was not purely luck.

But that had been before Her Husband came, and this was now. The colorful paperbacks on the desk's shelf smelled only like aging paper and more dust, with not one whiff of Morwen's scent. Granted they hadn't been of much use to her even when she'd been practicing, but these cheap, mass-produced grimoires had at least been a starting point. I'd appreciated that these books had encouraged her to involve me in rituals as her familiar. More than once I had, perhaps, been able to nudge a spell or two in the right direction. But her magical career had ended almost as soon as it had begun, when she'd gotten her new job and met Her Husband. I doubted Morwen had even noted my assistance.

I touched a paw to the books, in a brief, bittersweet salute to old times, before crossing the remnants of the chalk circle, and following my own dusty footprints out the door. It was evident that the night-gaunts had not been summoned in response to anything Morwen had done. In all likelihood, given Libby's double sighting this morning, they were not targeting this house or family in particular. Whatever their business in Kingsport was, it had nothing to do with me and mine, and I was sleepily grateful for that.

Below, the TV still blared, and my baby still squalled. I would inspect him later, and give him the post-lunch bath he would almost certainly require. In the meantime, though, I would treat myself to a nap amidst the soft, milky-smelling clothes on the shelves of the baby's room. Her Husband would never know.

ELDRITCH

***

That was a good nap, but I had a better one that evening, in a basket full of baby blankets that had been shoved under an end table in the living room and subsequently forgotten for months. Safe in this secluded space, I'd ventured once more into the realms of dream; not, this time, to the sunset city, but to Ulthar.

Ulthar was a bustling town famous in the dreamworlds for its formidable felines. You see, there had been some unpleasantness many, many centuries ago, when a child's kitten was killed by a wicked old couple, and the child had called upon ancient and terrible gods to exact his vengeance. That vengeance had come in the form of a cat army that had—there's no delicate way to put it, really—devoured the old couple down to the littlest finger-bones. Hence the local law against the killing of cats.

So the cats of Ulthar are comfortable and sleek, and nap on the sun-warmed cobblestone roads, secure in the knowledge that the three-wheeled carts of Ulthar will steer carefully around. And in addition to hosting many cats of its own, Ulthar is a popular tourist destination for cats of all types, from a variety of worlds.

That night, I was one of those tourists. I was at the Arched Back Inn, which did not exactly cater to cats—Ulthar being, technically, a town for humanoids—but which was famously cat-friendly. The proprietor was a one-eyed man with side-whiskers and a soft spot for felines, and he not only permitted cats to lie upon his enormous stone hearth, but occasionally laid out bowls of rich cream, or small fish, or liver, or other such tasty treats.

As it was dusk, the Arched Back was crowded with both cats and people, but I didn't mind; I was being charmed by a cat named Solar, a handsome brute of a Tom nearly as big as I, with fluffy cream-colored fur and a rakishly ragged ear. Solar was a cat of Earth like myself, but he'd postponed his reentrance into the material realm, preferring to adventure in the more uncertain—but more exciting—worlds of dream. Judging by his vague memories of horse-drawn carriages and powdered wigs, Solar had been dodging his reincarnation for quite some time.

"But, you know, there are rumors Carter is still around," he said, "though I don't see how it's possible. The sunset city has gone to rack and ruin. He left it to the cats, of course—all right and proper—but it would hardly be in such a state if he was still living."

I dredged my memory. "Carter is the sorcerer the cats rescued from the lunar beasts, right? On the dark side of the moon?"

"Mm-hmm," Solar purred. "I was there. Good eating that day. Those big toad-looking beasts don't look tasty, but actually their flesh bears a *distinct* resemblance to chicken."

"Sounds like a good time," I said. My tail twitched with jealousy. I had always moved dutifully from one lifetime to the next, never questioning or attempting to avoid my repeated incarnations in Kingsport. Now I wondered if I wasn't missing out on the real fun.

"He led an army of ghouls, too," said Solar, making the face most cats make when ghouls are mentioned. "And took out the lunar beasts' base."

My ears rotated forward at the mention of ghouls, betraying

my interest. "He befriended both cats and ghouls?" I asked. "Odd. You'd think he'd pick one or the other."

"Carter was a clever man. Far more broad-minded than most humans, really. And a splendid dreamer of course." Solar flicked his tongue over his nose—a gesture not dissimilar to the way I've seen certain dramatic humans kiss the tips of their fingers. "But he's either dead, or so far gone into another dimension that he may as well be."

The mention of ghouls had reminded me of Tilly's suggestion. "Have you ever talked to a ghoul?"

That face again. "Carrion-eating monkey dogs aren't my idea of good companions." Solar paused, and pondered for a moment. The leaping flames cast strange shadows across his handsome, whiskered face. "In point of fact, I have, though."

"How did it go?"

Solar's ear swiveled backwards and forwards, as though he were listening to his own memories. "It must have been several decades ago, as Earthers reckon it. I was heading North, when I came across a whole pack of those little brown what-d'you-call…"

Solar's voice faded, and the entire image of the inn flickered and blinked. In seconds I could hear him no longer, though I could still see his massive frame silhouetted against the fire. What I could hear, though, was this:

…sick of your shit! Like I don't have enough going on, and then you… Morwen's voice faded away, then came crackling back with new ferocity. *Just, fuck you!*

"I have to go," I tried to tell Solar…

…but I was already gone.

Blinking, I sat up in my cozy basket of blankets, and nearly bumped my head against the underside of the end table.

The yelling was becoming progressively louder. As usual I couldn't understand anything Her Husband said, but Morwen's meaning shone through her replies, as clear as a cat's angry yowl.

... and the sitter quit, and then you come in here and...I don't care! I'm sick of putting up with your bullshit! Oh, really, why not?! Let's go ahead and talk about it. Yeah, let's just set everything on fire!

I slunk out from under the table and into the kitchen. Her Husband was against the counter, gripping its edge so hard his knuckles were white. Morwen faced him, her arms folded against her swollen belly. Tears were trickling down her face, but her chin was lifted fiercely. My baby sat in his high chair, preoccupied in his effort to pick up a piece of cereal, and therefore not paying any attention. Thank the stars for the myopia of the young.

Her Husband snapped something sharp, and I watched in astonishment as the words rippled through the air. I could actually *see* them as a red, winding current of anger, drifting like smoke. As I stared, the counter under his hand jumped sideways a smidge. It wasn't much, but it unbalanced him, and he had to catch himself. This provoked another angry outburst, and more crimson words that hung heavily between them.

They weren't reaching Morwen, though. The air around her vibrated, buzzing bee-like against her skin. The sound clearly irritated her; she constantly shifted her stance and shook her head, as if attempting to get water out of her ears. However, she did not appear conscious either of her discomfort, or of its source. She spat back at Her Husband, and the awful buzzing increased, until I could feel it in my own teeth. I noted with alarm that a darkness was sliding over her skin, a shadow that was not her own.

Needless to say, this was all highly irregular. I'd witnessed several fights between Morwen and Her Husband before, and they did not typically involve anything like That Which Cannot Be Seen. Really, I wasn't sure how they could *not* notice what was happening, but it seemed obvious that they were blind and deaf to their dilemma.

I had to attract their notice. Normally I would do this by darting like an idiot from the doorway directly over Her Husband's foot, which would provoke a startled yelp, a curse, and a reproving comment from Morwen. Given the tension in the atmosphere, that did not seem like the wisest course. They needed refocusing, not further angering.

In the brief silence, my baby banged his fist gleefully against his tray—which gave me an idea. I slunk around the edges of the kitchen until I was directly behind him in his high chair.

"Sorry about this, little one," I told him. He wasn't listening, of course.

Her Husband spoke again. The red mist in the air was hard to breathe, I could tell, because his chest rose and fell with increasing rapidity. Meanwhile, the buzzing around Morwen intensified yet again, becoming almost the shrill whine of a mosquito, and blurring the air around her so that I could hardly see her face.

Unsheathing my claws, I sank them into the baby's dangling, sock-covered foot. Not too deep, of course, but enough to make him yelp, and then to bawl: big, hearty, attention-getting sobs.

By the time Her Husband and Morwen looked, I was crouched beneath the chair with my front paws tucked innocently under my chest. Not that they had eyes for me, anyway—they were focused entirely upon their howling offspring.

Her Husband said something to Morwen, and for once I understood its thrust: *Look, you've upset our son!* He moved toward the high chair with his arms outstretched, stepping away from the blood-red, smoke-like aura of his anger. Morwen, for her part, burst into tears, turned, and fled up the stairs…leaving behind the dark vibration.

Both the red mist and the black buzz hung in the air, each with an empty, person-shaped space in their middles. Then, the entire kitchen flickered. The counter jumped back into its original place—I know, because I was watching it carefully—and all trace of strange phenomena disappeared. It was just a kitchen again.

Her Husband was lifting my baby out of his high chair. Balancing the boy on his hip, he began to sway back and forth, patting my baby on his back and making soothing sounds. Satisfied that my baby was taken care of, I crept out from under the chair and dashed up the stairs after Morwen.

She wasn't in her bedroom. Up the bare wooden stairs I bounded, and into the small attic with its steeply-angled roof and ticklish scent of dust.

Morwen sat on the floor, her back resting against her desk, her bare feet smudging the scarcely-there remains of the chalk circle. Her arms were wrapped around her belly, and the baby within. Though the black buzz had remained downstairs, she sobbed noisily, with such effort that she had to pause now and then to cough and gasp.

I rubbed lovingly against her legs and got a smack and a "Shoo!" for my pains. I didn't take it personally. Whether cat or human, one should not hold the irrational behavior of a pregnant female against her: they are beholden to deep, primal instincts, not the conventions of civilization. So I sat nearby and curled my tail around my legs, blinking in a friendly fashion at my distraught friend.

"We could curse him," I reminded her cheerfully. "That botanica two towns over sells everything we need for hotfoot powder. He'd be gone in a flash."

Morwen, of course, neither understood nor responded. I hadn't really been serious about it anyway. Deeply as I disliked Her Husband, I'd seen firsthand how happy he made Morwen—or, at least, how happy he usually made her. Today was obviously the exception. Given what I'd witnessed, however, I suspected he was not personally to blame.

Eventually Morwen wiped her eyes and beckoned to me, as I'd known she would. With a hearty purr I strode forward and stroked my cheek against her damp fingers.

"It's not your fault," I told her, as she leaned forward to pick me up. She deposited me in her lap and I settled down between her crossed legs, resting my chin upon her belly. From there I could look directly upward into Morwen's red, swollen eyes, and purr both to her, and to the little one within her, whose rapid heartbeat I could just barely discern.

"There's something wrong with this town," I explained between purrs. Morwen was looking at me, but her gaze was unfocused, and I knew she was neither truly seeing nor hearing. I told her anyway, hoping that some dribble of meaning might leak through the barrier between us. "There's something wrong with Kingsport right now. Time and space are out of joint, and nobody is sure why. You can't see it or feel it yourselves, but it's true."

Morwen sighed and fondled my ears. I went on. "You have to look, Morwen," I urged her. "You have to See That Which Cannot Be Seen. You have the power, I know you do, if you'd only *try*. If you don't, this is just going to happen again. And what if I'm not there to stop it? I can't be around *all* the time."

Her fingers dropped from my ears to my chin. My purr deepened when she found the itchy spot that exists under every cat's jaw. "I'm serious, Morwen," I insisted, even as my eyes drifted shut. "I'm going to do what I can, but it may not be enough. You need to wake up, Morwen." A thought occurred to me. I opened my eyes wide, as wide as they would go, and made direct eye contact. "You need to wake up, Morwen," I told her, as clearly as I possibly could. "Wake up. See what's happening, what's *really* happening, not just what you *think* you should see. Wake up so you can protect your babies."

Morwen frowned at me, and for a hopeful second, I believed I'd gotten through. Then her eyes unfocused again. I sighed and settled down into a steady purr, matching my rhythms to the wee heartbeat that fluttered against my chest.

She was never going to see.

5

Hideous

That night, I circled the bedrooms three times, checking to be sure that my baby, Morwen, and Her Husband were all asleep, and that nothing lingered in the house to disturb their slumber. I also freshened a few sigils I'd carved in the baseboards, ones that Her Husband had previously varnished over. Claws thus sharpened, I finally felt safe in leaving the house for my nightly rounds. With luck I could do a spot of hunting, too. Morwen had bought the shrimp-flavored kibble again—my least favorite—so my diet required supplementation.

The grass was frosty and cold on my paws, and I could smell snow in the air. Heavy clouds hung low, reflecting the city's lights and turning the whole sky a luminous rose-gray. Pretty though the sight was, it was far from ideal hunting light. I reached the row of tall pines that bordered my yard, resigned to a depressing dinner of flavorless crunchies, when I suddenly scented blood.

I slunk around one broad trunk, and beheld a dim white figure crouched, half-hidden, behind the next tree in the row.

At the same time, her scent reached me, as did a heavier whiff of the meaty aroma. I straightened up and trotted forward.

"How did you get *that*?" I asked Dot admiringly.

Dot's back arched and she jumped, startled by the sound of my voice. I laughed as her fur settled back into position. She glared at me over her shoulder, one paw still on the dove she'd been devouring. There was a small gray feather dangling out of the corner of her mouth, making her adorably squashed face even more comical than usual.

"It flew right into me," she said. "Like it didn't see me. Even in this light."

"Huh. Doves don't usually do that," I said.

"Nothing has been right today."

"You noticed?"

She dipped her head sagely, and the feather drifted off, to rest in the snow. "You can have some," she added generously.

"Thanks," I said. "Morwen's been budgeting again."

Dot shuddered delicately and moved aside, so that I could join her at the unexpected feast. She'd been working at the back, and a whole swath of good, red meat was exposed. I thrust my face in and chewed, working a bit of muscle around until it tore free and I could resurface to swallow. Then it was Dot's turn. As we ate, it began to snow—big, white, drifting flakes that soon hid the bloody smears left by the downed bird.

"So what's happening?" Dot asked at last. She was gnawing on the bird's head, and I could hear the skull crunch between her teeth. "What's making it all weird?"

"I'm not sure," I said. "According to Tilly, the night-gaunts Libby and I have been seeing are just symptoms, not the cause."

Dot paused in her loud munching, her already large green eyes growing rounder. "Libby saw a night-gaunt?" she asked in surprise.

"Two," I told her. "Around his house."

Dot resumed chewing, and I watched upper vertebrae disappear between her lips. She swallowed, hard. "I saw something else," she volunteered.

"You have blood on your cheeks," I interrupted. Leaning forward, I started to lick one side clean, pressing firmly on her fluffy fur with every stroke of my tongue. I knew white was a bitch to maintain—I'd had a white coat myself several lives ago. As I proceeded, her purr rumbled faintly in her chest.

"Well, I didn't *see*," Dot clarified drowsily, lulled half-asleep by the feast and the grooming. "I *smelled*."

I paused, and spoke without thinking. "Fish. You smelled something fishy, but it wasn't fish. It was something else."

Dot opened her eyes, cocking her head in curiosity. "How did you *know*?"

I didn't answer. I'd felt it in my gut, that was how—deep down, by the base of the spine, far from my chattering consciousness. That was where intuition lived, and right now it twisted my stomach into foreboding knots.

The air suddenly hung heavy with potential, and even the small, squeaking and fluttering things of the night paused in their various flights. The universe was listening. Things were happening. The tiny individual pieces of a cosmos-wide puzzle were gently snapping themselves into place.

I'd encountered this sensation before. It's good news when you're the one casting spells in the attic, twirling the delicate threads of reality around your claws. It's bad news when you're at the other end of those threads, and someone is yanking your life askew.

Dot did not seem conscious of the night's enchantment;

perhaps it was all in my head. Even so, that moment offered the nudge I'd needed. Whoever was stirring the pot in Kingsport, I fully intended to shove my own ladle in.

"Will you dream with me?" I asked Dot.

She was chewing the bloodied fur between her toes, and shot me a dubious look over her extended claws. "What, now? Here?"

"Yes."

"It's cold," she complained.

"It's important."

"You think everything's important," she grumbled, already getting to her feet.

We slunk beneath the low-hanging branches and discovered, at the base of the tree, a little snow-free hollow within a thick bed of fallen needles. It was a bit prickly, but when we curled up together it was warm, and the fir's heady aroma lulled us into a deep winter's sleep.

* * *

Together we traversed the formless forest that bounded the deeper dreamlands, but this time we did not enter the sunset city of the cats, nor any of the better-traveled realms. Instead I led Dot to a different place, one I hadn't visited in years.

We leapt up a long, spiraling staircase, and emerged at ground level, under a dim, foggy sun. The ground was wet and cold, and the coarse grass dampened our bellies with dew. Somehow everything contrived to smell of frog, though there wasn't a single frog in sight.

We'd arrived amidst the ruins of an ancient settlement; here and there in the mist the tumbled remains of stone buildings were just visible. The best-preserved, a half-collapsed gray temple, still stood guard over the rest. One column slanted sideways across its entrance, propping up the leaning remains of the walls, and from this dangled thick clumps of swamp moss, an emerald curtain concealing the mysteries.

Under this column and through this moss I slunk, shaking the wet off my paws at every step. The temple was as deserted as I'd recalled, and appeared not to have changed at all in the intervening years—though the passage of time is always uncertain in the dreamlands. By local standards it might have been mere weeks since my last visit. It might also have been several hundred years.

At any rate, there was the divining pool, built upon a star-shaped platform at the exact center of the room. The steps leading up to it were broken, but I simply jumped to the wide ledge that surrounded the sacred waters, and peered within.

Though the ceiling was open above me, the pool did not reflect the gray sky, or the sun that struggled to shine between heavy clouds. The waters were black, save for the occasional faint twinkle far, far down in their depths. Was it a star? The slight glow of a tiny, phosphorescent fish? I certainly didn't know. I didn't even know how far down the water went, and whether this was a shallow, black-painted pool, or a well of unimaginable proportions.

Curling my tail around my paws, I studied my own reflection, which was eerily clear in the dark surface. I was aware of Dot taking a seat beside me, but I stayed focused upon my reflection; curiously, though she was right beside me, I could not see hers.

"Spirits of the temple and of prophecy," I intoned, underlying my words with my throatiest purr. "I command you, by the One and the Many, and by the barbarous names of old. By the gods and spirits of the one hundred and eight realms, by the white light and the red, I conjure you to obey me. Nor will you find my words without value, my promises unkept, or my offerings unworthy of your great and particular powers." I paused and considered the phrasing of my question. "How do I discover what's amiss in Kingsport? And how can I best protect my friends and family, both human and feline, in the days to come?" Leaning forward, I awaited the response.

There were shadows in the pool, and strange, gleaming reflections upon its surface. I let my gaze soften, so that my own reflected face appeared blurred and hazy.

The vision I saw could have been in the pool, or in my own mind—or perhaps both. It was snowing rather heavily; enormous, fluffy flakes continually crossed my line of sight. Vividly I perceived a granite tombstone to my left, and a broken stone cross not far from me, perhaps ten body-lengths ahead. There hung a foul reek of ghoul in the air—half dog, half rot. I glimpsed motion far away: a white shape loped up a tombstone-strewn hill, and disappeared into the woods beyond.

With a blink, the mirage vanished. I shook my head, trying to get the cobwebs out of my brain, and turned to Dot, who was thoroughly licking her fluffy white tail.

"How long was I out?" I asked.

Dot paused, considered. "A twentieth part of the night?" she ventured, calculating time in the old feline fashion. "Did it work?"

"I think so," I said. "I was in a graveyard. There was—" I shuddered. "There was a ghoul."

"Which graveyard?" Dot wanted to know.

"One of the ones in Kingsport, I hope. It looked quite old. But I can't be sure until I get there. I've never been to any graveyards in this lifetime. Have you?"

"Not *in* one," said Dot. "Not in Kingsport. Too many ghouls." She paused her grooming abruptly. "Was it in town?"

"By the edge. Next to a wood, or at least a patch of trees."

"That'd be Burying Hill. You know where that is?"

"Of course." Actually I had only a vague idea, but I couldn't tell that to *Dot*. Dot hunted a larger territory than any molly I knew, and possessed an almost disconcerting ability to navigate it. I'd look a right fool to her if I couldn't find such a long-established location as Burying Hill.

Giving her tail a last lick, Dot sprang from the ledge to the broken tiles below. "We'd better go, then," she called over her shoulder, as she stalked toward the entrance. "Because clearly you have a hair up your ass about this whole thing, and aren't going to give any of us any peace until you figure it out."

"Bite me," I suggested. I stretched myself in a bow before the spirits of the pool. "Should your visions lead me right," I muttered, "I promise rewards both rapid and rich. Go in peace."

With a final flick of my tail I dismissed the unseen beings, and followed Dot into the semi-sunshine of the swamp outside.

"Let's go find Cinnamon and tell her to meet us outside the graveyard," Dot suggested.

My tail lashed, betraying my feelings. "Why her? Let's get Libby."

"Both would be better," said Dot. "And what's your problem with Cinnamon, anyway? She's huge—she doesn't even look like a housecat. I bet she'd give a ghoul pause."

I'm just as big! I could give a ghoul pause! I wanted to retort. Then it occurred to me that if the de-clawed Cinnamon tried to defend us from a ghoul, there was a good chance she'd get eaten. That consoled me a little. "Fine," I agreed. "Why don't you find them in the dreamlands, and tell them to wake up and meet us just outside the graveyard. I'll go scope it out first, and see if it's the same one as in my vision. No point in us risking our lives for the wrong graveyard."

"You shouldn't go alone," said Dot. "That's the point of getting Libby and Cinnamon. The more bodies the better." She paused. "I shouldn't have used the word 'bodies.'"

"It was unfortunate," I agreed. "Don't worry, I'm just going to climb a good tree and look it over. I'll wait for you before I do anything."

Before Dot could protest further or, worse, rethink the whole crazy idea, I woke up.

* * *

Despite the shelter of the fir, there was a fine layer of snow upon our fur. I laid a friendly lick across Dot's ear before easing out of the nest we'd made. My muscles were stiff, and my very bones creaked as I stretched. Dot slept on, snuffling through her squashed nose.

Cautiously, I peered out from under the tree. A cold, dry snow continued to fall, coating the grass with a thin white blanket that glittered beneath the lustrous sky. There was nothing to see, even when I looked for That Which Cannot Be Seen, so I bounded forward in search of Burying Hill. If I remembered its location correctly, it was also on the west side of Kingsport, but towards the northern edge of the town.

At this time of night, and in this season, the streets were deserted. The windows of every house were dark. In front of them, the old wrought-iron street lamps shed golden cones of light, illuminating wide expanses of sparkling, untouched snow, and the occasional parked car. The lazily drifting snow promised to fill in the footprints I left in gardens, across yards, and on the tops of fences as I worked my way across town.

Some graveyards are devoured by the living, surrounded by new construction as the population relentlessly swells. Not so this one. Kingsport had expanded in another direction, and left this city of the dead alone. Burying Hill's presiding church had burned a decade ago; its black timbers still cluttered its stone foundation, for no one had bothered to rebuild it. The graveyard felt unguarded, abandoned, without the civilizing influence of the church and its bells. It was bordered by forest, and dotted with ancient, massive oaks, which despite their great size swayed even in this gentle wind. I knew why, because I knew who had riddled this place with their tunnels, and gnawed hungrily at the trees' roots until they could barely stand upright.

With all this in mind, I chose a young, slender tree that grew where the churchyard ended and the graveyard began. It was not a very good place to hide, without any concealing leaves, but I clawed my way to a sufficient height to avoid being attacked, and settled along what was—I hoped—a sufficiently thick branch for my weight. While getting comfortable, I spotted a tiny headstone directly below me: an infant's long-forgotten grave.

Relaxing a little, I unfocused my eyes, and opened my

internal vision to That Which Cannot Be Seen. Immediately the graveyard took on a...*different* appearance. It was filled with half-seen blurs of movement, sometimes drifting between the tilted headstones, sometimes concentrated upon the graves. Each was a mere light-dispelling fog until I focused upon it, and every time I did, I shuddered.

A few local spirits, in shapes neither human nor animal, hovered at the edge of the forest; they might linger halfway between this world and the dreamlands, but their sharp white teeth seemed material enough.

A vampire—not the Dracula sort, the real kind—was rising from her grave, drifting like mist to assemble herself above the ground. She stretched white, bare arms to the moonlight and sniffed the air with vigor; when she looked over her shoulder, it was at me. She smiled, and it wasn't friendly. Then she vanished, and was not even a shadow amongst the many.

The hair stood all along my spine, and I fought the urge to hiss or, at least, to look over my shoulder, and see if she was there...

A sob from below distracted me. The moonlight wavered just beneath the tree; when I Saw That Which Cannot Be Seen, a phantom lingered there, weeping bitterly upon the infant's grave. The hair eased along my back, even as my guts churned to hear the raw grief in her sobs. How long ago had her baby died? How long ago had she? Yet still, some fragment of her soul—wherever the rest was now—lingered in this graveyard, trapped by its pattern of sorrow. The ghost looked up in my direction, but I could see no recognition in her filmy eyes. Whatever dimension she inhabited, it was just adjacent to mine; our worlds could only slide blindly past each other, like unlit ships on a moonless night.

It's a feline gift, to glimpse so many realms from where we perch within our own. Humans once could do the same—how else could they have learned so much, in such a short time?—but the ability appeared to be waning. So too were the rituals and propitiations and secret teachings that held our dimension together at the seams. I had seen for myself how the spirit world grew bolder and bolder, operating without fear in a population turned increasingly blind and deaf...

My depressing ruminations were brought to an end by a sudden, soundless flurrying. Spirits drifted back into the shadows of the trees; ghosts faded away into nothingness. Even the grieving mother glanced back over her shoulder with sudden, perceptive fear, and blinked away as swiftly as she'd appeared. I narrowed my eyes in the direction she'd stared, awaiting the approach of whatever being could clear the graveyard by its mere presence.

An unholy beast loped between the gravestones. It looked rather like a hairless dog, with four long limbs and rubbery gray skin, which bounced disgustingly as it ran. Its nose was black, and its teeth were long, white, and sharp. But as much as I hate dogs, that wasn't the terrible part.

What made it hideous was that, as much as the beast resembled a dog, even more did it resemble a man. Its powerful jaw was thrust forward in terrible parody of a muzzle, the tip of its nose was black, and its pointed ears turned in all directions—dog-like enough, you might say. Yet the face was unmistakably the blue-eyed, flat-nosed remnants of something once human.

The creature slowed and then stood, rearing up on its hind legs with uncanny ease. Now the front paws were revealed to be hands, albeit horribly clawed, with black nails like the talons of some wicked bird. Other bits were revealed too—ghouls, despite their semi-human origins, didn't believe in clothes. The ghoul sniffed the air, and I kept utterly still, praying to the many saints of cats that he would not notice me. I was downwind, which was a distinct advantage, but a Maine Coon isn't easy to hide.

A powerful blow struck the tree from behind, knocking me loose. My claws sank deep into the wood of the branch, but my weight had already shifted too far. I watched, almost in slow motion, as my claws slid across the bark, leaving long, white, futile marks in their wake. Then I fell.

That, too, seemed to take a long time—but I landed on my feet. And not just on my feet, but with my fangs bared and claws swiping, yowling a war-cry designed to deafen any opponent.

All for nought. I was instantly swept sideways by a single, devastating blow. I landed badly on my side, and had no time to recover my breath, for the creature was upon me, his unnatural muzzle almost touching my own.

It was a ghoul, of course, but this one was some sort of albino. The eyes that glared into mine were a hazy pink, and the bristling brows above them were white. So pale was his skin that it was nearly fish-belly green, particularly in the moonlight. Even the crooked teeth that thrust past his lower lip gleamed like ivory. To my shock, I recognized him: the white, distant, loping figure I'd glimpsed in my dreamlands vision. I had found the object of my quest. It was definitely the right graveyard, after all.

But there was no time to ask questions, for it was clear that he intended to ask none. Already his open jaws were descending. He was going to pull my head right off my shoulders, and crunch my skull between his teeth. I had done the same to mice.

Now there was no more thought. At the last moment, my claws lashed out and broke the monotony of his albino face with two long, dark streaks of blood. He reared back and licked his nose with an almost indignant air, never breaking eye contact with me. His paw wasn't holding me down—he merely stood above me—but I did not twist to regain my feet and flee. Should I turn my back for even a moment, I knew he would bite with crushing force upon my exposed spine. Instead, I abruptly curled forward, to bite him sharply upon his unprotected neck.

He yelped with surprise, then snarled, a hideous sound that made my teeth meet each other in a paroxysm of terror. Another yelp as my jaws pierced those rubbery folds, and I felt him clawing frantically at my shoulder, tearing into my flesh with those awful talons, trying to pull me from his neck. My face was buried in the pale flesh but I swiped blindly, frantically, with my left paw, aiming for his eyes. Another howl told me I'd hit something good, but at that moment he'd seized my neck with his stubby fingers, and I could neither think nor breathe. Blood pounded in my head, and all was red behind my eyes.

He jolted sideways, and I was released. I twisted and rolled, landing on my feet. Everything was spots for long, long seconds, but then they began to clear, and I could peer dizzily through the haze.

My savior was Cinnamon, currently squaring off against the ghoul who, though he still dwarfed the young Savannah cat, seemed reluctant to engage with something that appeared so wild.

"Spice! This way!" Dot called from my right. I ran half-blind in the direction of her voice, my head and my shoulder pounding. At last my vision fully returned, and I saw her and Libby crouched in the grass at the edge of the graveyard. They sprinted away as soon as I neared, and I followed them as fast as I could. I could smell the blood oozing from my shoulder, but the limb still worked, and that was all that mattered.

Sounds in the grass behind me. I half-turned, ready to face the ghoul again. Instead I saw Cinnamon on my tail in a flat-out run and, some distance behind us both, the albino ghoul, racing along on all fours. An eerie sound split the night, something that might have been a laugh or a howl; it echoed around the gravestones, coming from here, there, everywhere. A loathsome grey face popped up from one of the many hidden tunnels, and watched the albino chase us with a tongue-lolling grin. The ghouls evidently found the rout of their friend amusing.

But the albino ghoul wasn't laughing, and neither were we. It was the size of a man, with legs like a greyhound, and we were but four housecats. I didn't need to look behind me to know that it was gaining.

We were now in the town proper, racing across the snow-slick pavement of a new housing development. A man stepping out of his car paused to stare at the rapid procession of cats. In the brief glimpse I caught of his puzzled face, I never saw his eyes track toward the ghoul. Why would he see it? Ghouls were but one of the many Things Which Cannot Be Seen. It was a real, physical being whose hot breath I fancied I could feel on my tail, but to this inexperienced human he simply didn't exist—and if there were any footprints left, they would be dismissed as those of some oversized dog, romping in the snowfall.

An open storm drain yawned ahead, a black rectangle in the snow-covered sidewalk. Libby passed it—so did Dot—Cinnamon crowded me on my right. I risked a glance over my shoulder, and stared almost directly into the mad, red eyes of the slavering ghoul. With no conscious thought I steered away from my friends and dove down the dark, reeking hole.

Splash. I was in frigid water up to my belly. The pain of my sudden, icy immersion almost outdid the growing throbbing in my shoulder—but I thought he wouldn't follow.

I'd miscalculated. A much more massive form than mine momentarily blocked the opening, shutting out all light and landing me in darkness. I was already moving by the time he splashed down beside me…but to where? Down the watery tunnels would be suicide—the ghoul was sure to catch me!

There! A long pole, possibly once belonging to a rake or snow shovel, leaned against the sewer wall. How had it gotten there? Perhaps some curious kids had been poking into the storm drain with it. I didn't know, and I didn't care. I was halfway up it before its presence had even registered in my conscious mind. The ghoul snapped at my heels, and I launched myself—I believed I actually levitated—toward that distant rectangle of light.

I was clawing at the pavement. Two front paws only, then a hind paw, then I was squirming away from the opening, with barely a memory of how I'd gotten there. I looked back, and my heart sank to see a white, coarse-skinned hand emerge, feeling its way outward for a better grip on the pavement. The tall ghoul could reach the opening, and was going to haul himself up. I staggered away, looking for some tree, fence, or human—anything, really—that I could clamber up to save my soaking-wet skin.

But I had forgotten my friends. Cinnamon leapt to my defense, in a lovely motion like an angry cheetah, and growled down the grate. Dot followed and scratched violently at the ghoul's groping hand, which withdrew with a muffled curse and a snarl.

"Just try it," Cinnamon hissed, and aimed a blow at the darkness, evidently as a sample. A pity she was declawed—hopefully, the threat wouldn't be tested.

Libby circled cautiously around the storm drain, and came to check on me. "You're bleeding a lot," he told me. "And you're all wet."

"I-I-I-I k-k-k-know, you idiot."

"Don't you 'idiot' me," he admonished, sniffing at my injured shoulder. "I'm not the one who went wandering alone in a ghoul-infested graveyard."

Too tired to argue, I settled for purring feebly as Libby licked the wound, and tried not to wince at his rough tongue.

"You feline morons," the ghoul snarled. His speech was in a language common to the dreamlands, but thick-lipped and oddly cadenced. "You think I don't know these tunnels like the back of my hand? I'll follow them all over the town, and sniff you and your humans out."

"Please. You ghouls only eat the dead. A proper hunt is beyond you," Dot said with a growl.

"I'll make an exception! I'll…" The ghoul's voice trailed off abruptly.

After a long moment, Cinnamon coughed. "You'll do… what?" she prompted helpfully.

There was no answer. Dot sniffed, sneezed, and abruptly straightened up.

"Spice!" she called to me. "It's that fish smell again."

A sharp whine cut across her words; I almost couldn't catch what she said.

"It's a Deep One!" the ghoul yelped. "Let me up, let me up! Pax, I call pax!"

Libby was still assiduously licking my shoulder, but I limped forward, shivering so violently I could hardly speak.

"Wh-what i-is a-a D-d-deep O-one?" I stammered. Dot took one look at my condition and pressed bravely against me, despite my wet, stinky fur; Cinnamon too snuggled close. Warmth spread slowly but surely across my sides, and I took my first deep breath in a long time.

"Never mind! Let me out, now!"

"W-we'll let you up," I said slowly, "but you have to tell us something."

"Up! Up!" the ghoul demanded. His hands emerged once again from the dark, the black claws scraping across the pavement, but Dot struck swiftly, and with another yelp they withdrew. "Quickly! Please!"

"Wh-why did the ghouls bring the night-gaunts?" I managed to get out with hardly a tremor.

"The night-gaunts? What—oh!"

"Tell us," I demanded.

"Let me up first!"

The fishy reek grew stronger. Was it my imagination, or did I hear sloshing footsteps below? The ghoul whined again, a long, drawn-out sound.

"Tell us," was all I said.

"It was the monster," the ghoul gibbered. "The white thing on the island in the pond. Black's Pond! It wanted us to bring the night-gaunts! We made a deal, we did our part, take it up with that thing, the one in the pond! Please!"

"Let him up," I told Dot. Dot shot me a glare like I'd ordered her to abandon a three-legged rat. I must have looked serious about it, because when I backed slowly from the entrance, she and Cinnamon followed.

In far less time than I'd have expected the ghoul hauled himself out, squeezing painfully through the narrow hole in the curb. He crouched before us, panting and shivering, and I held my breath while he glowered at us with pink, blood-streaked eyes.

But in the end, he only sneered, pale lips curling upward to reveal polished fangs. "Take it up with the thing in the pond," he repeated, and with a last fearful glance over his shoulder at the storm drain, loped away.

The fish smell was now eye-wateringly potent, and the four of us did not wait to see if the Deep One would pursue its lost prey. We scampered away ourselves, and did not rest until we were once again in familiar territory, under a pine at the corner of Wood and Jefferson, not far from any of our homes.

"The island in the middle of Black's Pond," I repeated. "Do any of you know what he means?"

"No," said Dot, and Cinnamon shook her head, but Libby spoke up at once.

"It's a bit of a landmark, actually. Some sort of crazy old hermit lived in a shack there or something. Tourists ask about it sometimes, but nobody ever goes."

"What about the monster? 'A white thing'—isn't that what he said?"

"I don't know," said Libby. "But really, nobody goes there, ever. We had a painter once who was just dying to get on the island and paint the pond from that perspective, but she never could find anyone with a boat to take her over, or even someone to lend her a pair of waders. It was like she was… blocked, if you know what I mean."

I did. We all did. Sometimes, things don't happen for a reason—and that reason is not always within our comprehension. "Well, we'll have to find a way over," I said.

"Why?" Dot wanted to know. But before I could answer, she cut me off. "Ugh, forget it. Spice, you're all torn up and you smell ungodly and you're likely to freeze in this weather. Go home. I'll talk sense into you some other night."

"I want to go," Cinnamon volunteered. This was evidently her good-bye, for she nudged against me with a little purr, and slunk out from under the pine tree with no further ado.

"I *don't*," said Libby emphatically.

"What if Mark and Clarence are in danger?" I wanted to know. "What if whatever-it-is means to destroy the whole town?"

Libby's ears flattened, and his nose wrinkled into a troubled expression. "I don't know," he eventually concluded unhappily. "Let's…let's just see."

"Go *home,* Spice," Dot told me sharply. She bumped against my shoulder in a way that was hardly friendly at all. "Before Morwen has to take you to the vet."

"She's going to take me anyway," I muttered.

"Oh!" said Libby cheerfully, as I slipped cautiously out from under the pine and back into the white wonderland of the streets. "So *that's* why you don't want to go home. Well, good luck!"

6

Spectral

As I'd expected, Morwen lost her shit when she discovered me in the kitchen the next morning. I was still pretty well torn up, but the bleeding had stopped and I didn't smell half so bad as before—so what was all the fuss about? But my protests were ignored. Her Husband went to work, a new babysitter was summoned early, and I was bundled into that awful cat carrier and placed in the front seat of Morwen's rattling car.

Honestly, Pumpkin Spice, why now? Morwen moaned, while she slid her big-bellied self, with difficulty, into the driver's seat. The grumbling didn't stop as she backed out of the driveway, though my comprehension of it waned as Morwen went into specifics. To be honest I wasn't paying very much attention. I get carsick, and I was staring glassily through the cat carrier's little grate, trying to abate the nausea. If I crammed my head against the door and looked past Morwen, I could see a bit of passing scenery through the driver-side window, and that helped.

Briefly, but without warning, the entire world went transparent. The car and the cat carrier alike turned a filmy, see-through gray. I yowled at the sight of *nothing* between me and the passing asphalt, and scrambled frantically for purchase on the invisible floor—only to yowl again as the asphalt transformed into bumpy cobblestones.

Over my own panicked squalls, I caught a horse's shrill neigh. I looked up to see a horse rearing over my head, its spectral hooves descending through the shadowy roof of the car.

What the—oh my God! Morwen yelled, and slammed on the brakes. The car shuddered, swerved, and crashed. The carrier flew forward and smacked directly into the dash. I shrieked with shock as I collided w the hard plastic. My head hit, and for long seconds all I could see were stars.

By the time everything stopped spinning, the carrier rested on its side on the passenger floorboard. From where it lay, I couldn't see Morwen. Was she hurt? Was the baby all right? I meowed, at first tentatively, then more vigorously.

Why didn't she answer?

The carrier shook slightly from a small impact. Pat, pat, pat went a hand on top of the plastic roof. *It's ok*, I understood Morwen to say. *It's ok, baby. Are you all right?*

I howled a joyful affirmative. She rotated the carrier so the door was on top, tumbling me with it, but I was too relieved to complain. Unlatching the grate, Morwen reached a soothing hand inside to stroke me. I purred and nuzzled my nose into her shaking fingers.

Multiple humans outside the car window shouted and called, and Morwen answered in a voice as shaky as her hand. The car door opened, and one or two angry voices stopped at once. Instead, I listened as a concerned female human took over. She I could understand quite clearly—she must've had cats herself.

Let's get you to a doctor, honey.

With the carrier standing on its end, it was difficult to see, but I assumed the ensuing shuffling sounds were of other humans helping Morwen from the car. I could also tell, from the street sounds, that they'd left the car door open. After a long pause, during which nobody came to fetch me, I squirmed my way up out of the carrier. Easing my bruised self down to the floor, I crouch half-hidden on the floorboard in front of the driver's seat. From there, I could observe the scene at my leisure.

A small crowd of people surrounded Morwen, who was tearful and upset but who, as far as I could tell, did not smell of blood. None of them were looking my way, but it was only a matter of time before Morwen remembered my presence, and then I'd be forcibly returned to the carrier.

And after that? I'd be taken to the vet and likely locked up for days, unable to either comfort or protect poor Morwen. Meanwhile, these time-slips would likely continue, if not intensify, placing all of us in immediate danger. Was I content to remain trapped in a cage, useless to all, while my friends and my hometown suffered? I was not.

So I hated to do it…but it really was for the best. Staying low and moving slow, I oozed out the driver side door and slunk underneath the car. When I'd reached the far side of the car's protective shadow, I bolted across the (thankfully empty) street, and sprinted down the first alley I encountered.

Morwen would be terribly upset when she discovered me gone. But not as upset as she'd be if this whole cursed town fell apart.

* * *

I'd gotten almost no sleep the night before. My shoulder was torn, and throbbing all the way down to my paw. I was limping through the snow. I had just been in a car wreck caused by a bizarre temporal shift the likes of which I'd never witnessed, in any lifetime.

So I was not at my best when I ran into the King.

The cat King of the neighborhood was sprawled upon his house's old porch swing, dangling his head over the faded, splintery edge to casually observe his domain. His tail twitched and slapped the wood as I slunk past; though his ears swiveled my way, he said nothing. I thought I was off the hook when, just as I prepared to cross the street, he hailed me.

"You. Pumpkin Spice. Where are you going in that condition?"

My ears flattened as I reluctantly turned back.

The King sprang from his place on the swing, setting it rocking and creaking back and forth, back and forth. He sauntered up to me and sniffed my shoulder in a curious way. Though here he wasn't the great panther he was in the dreamlands, he was still a brawny tuxedo tom, nearly as big as I was—no mean feat for a mere short-haired domestic.

"You'll bring dogs down on us," he observed. "Or worse—foxes. Go home and wash so you don't reek of blood."

"Sorry, Your Highness," I replied stiffly, trying to force my ears into a more friendly, or at least less pissed-off, position. "I can't just yet."

Languidly the King raised his gaze. His eyes were a brilliant, poisonous green, hypnotic in their clarity. Two centuries ago, he'd have been thrown into the fire as a witch's familiar, for his black fur and those eyes.

"Why?" he asked simply.

"There's something wrong with this town," I said, and could not entirely hide my irritation. Hadn't he noticed? What sort of King couldn't keep tabs on his kingdom?

"Oh?"

"Some sort of temporal dislocation," I said briefly. "Two different times overlapped. It caused my human to wreck her car, nearly killing us both. I aim to stop it."

I must have finally surprised him, because his pupils widened, turning nearly round. Then they narrowed again, as his characteristic superciliousness overpowered his interest. "How? Alone, and looking like *that*?" He sat, confident in his condescension, and curled his tail around his toes. "Whatever spirits are working this town, they'll certainly be able to smell you coming. And even if they didn't, what could you possibly do to stop them? Whoever they are, these are powerful entities—maybe even the Neighbors themselves." He scratched the snow, forming a Mark against evil, as all cats do when forced to mention them. "*They're* not likely to be swayed by a kitty."

"It's not 'entities,' it's 'entity,'" I retorted. "Whatever lives on the island in the middle of Black's Pond."

The King's eyes narrowed, and I caught his tail twitching. "How do you know?"

This was a bit of a sticking point. I bent down and casually, briefly groomed my good leg, to show I didn't care what I was about to admit. "A ghoul told me."

"A ghoul?" I was still deeply engaged in examining the short hairs on my foreleg, but I could *hear* the King's nose wrinkle. "Why on Earth would you talk to a ghoul? And why would it tell you the truth?"

"It was in…straitened circumstances," I told him demurely,

studying my paw, as if too humble to describe how I'd overpowered and threatened a full-grown ghoul. "And I can't see that it had any reason to lie."

Giving my paw a last nibble, I looked up. Rather to my surprise, the King's gaze was distant. Thoughtful.

"It won't be easy to get on that island," he volunteered. "There's a deception around it. I don't think whatever lives there likes to be disturbed."

"I have my ways," I said airily.

"So do I," he said. Rising quickly, without even a good preparatory stretch, he nosed open the cracked front door and strolled purposefully inside.

I dithered on the front stoop, uncertain whether to follow or to leave—had I been invited or dismissed? The King saved me from social awkwardness by reappearing as suddenly as he'd left. He was carrying something between his jaws—what, precisely, I couldn't say.

"Here," he said, without ado, and dropped the object at my feet.

It was a paw-sized hunk of rusted, corroded iron in the rough shape of a key; I describe it that way because, whatever it had once been, it certainly hadn't been an actual, working key. Likely it had been intended as an amulet, especially given the large hoop it made at one end, through which was tied a leather string that looked nearly as dirty and old as the amulet itself. What was more, the entire thing reeked—and I mean *reeked*—of tom-cat piss.

"This is one of the kingdom's treasures," the King volunteered, licking his lips with something of a grimace. "Passed from King to King for millennia. I was told it hailed originally from Scandinavia, and came to England in the mouth of a mighty King of Forest Cats, long before it made its way to this New World." The King nudged the amulet with his paw. "It should open a way for you to the island."

"Thank you," I said, shocked into genuine gratitude. "I'm sure it will be useful."

The King's eyes narrowed with sleepy disinterest—the cat equivalent, I suppose, of a human being's shrug. "Bring it back when you're done," he said. "If you live," he added, before leaping back upon his porch swing, and setting it once more rocking and creaking from rusted chains.

I almost asked if he cared to come too, before realizing that I had no desire for him to join me whatsoever. Still, it was odd, to loan a treasure like this so casually, when the chances of it being returned were far from certain. Of course, it was not the first time I had found the King too cavalier in his duties, but it did make me wonder…

With an effort I bit the precious amulet, trying not to touch its urine-encrusted surface with my tongue, and carried it away. I did look back over my shoulder, considering that, perhaps, this was a trick of some kind—but the King was already dozing in the winter sun once more, his head dangling crookedly off the side of the ancient swing.

* * *

"It's disgusting!" said Libby, wrinkling his nose.

"It's *powerful*," muttered Cinnamon, sniffing it with care.

"It's from the King?" Dot narrowed her eyes suspiciously.

One by one I had fetched my fellow cats, laboriously walking—in broad daylight!—to each of their houses to summon them in person, as it was still too early in the morning to trust that they could be found in the dreamlands. We were now gathered by Black's Pond, directly in front of the island that was, apparently, causing all this trouble. This was not exactly prime cat territory; the low banks were too marshy for our liking, and the high banks had a tendency to crumble away without much warning. Dot had previously sworn that, in summer, this area was good hunting, but she was a fanatic; the rest of us would rather eat kibble than venture this far from town, and this close to so much water.

Those were mere practical considerations: there were other reasons to dislike the place. Such as the white mist that still hung around the low island, long past the time it should have been burned off by the sun.

"Why give it to you?" Dot went on distrustfully. "If he has the ability to fix this problem, he ought to do it himself. It's *his* responsibility."

"Heavy lies the head upon which rests a crown," Libby murmured poetically.

"Well, for whatever reason, he's not. So it's up to us," I told them firmly. I had already told them about the car accident and its circumstances, and so no one was willing to argue. I might be a trifle more protective of my humans than the average cat, but Libby and Dot, I knew, were also fond of their people. Cinnamon's family I didn't know much about, beyond that they were both rich enough to afford a Savannah, and old-fashioned enough to let her roam; yet Cinnamon had required the least persuasion of them all. I put it down to her kittenish energy.

"Damn good thing the pond's frozen," Libby muttered,

pointedly loud enough for me to hear. "Or she'd have us swimming, too!"

"How does it work?" Cinnamon wanted to know.

I realized I wasn't sure. With true cat ingenuity, I endeavored to conceal that as much as possible. "Why don't you give it a go first, Cinnamon," I said vaguely, licking my paw and passing it over my ear in a casual way. "We'll follow along behind." As soon as I'd delivered the command, I twisted round and fell to licking my haunch, to further demonstrate how much I didn't care, and also to keep my mouth busy so that no one would expect me to talk.

I heard the dull clack of metal on teeth as Cinnamon picked up the powerful (and disgusting) talisman, then the swish of her tail as it swept through the tall grass. I also heard Dot pad closer to me, on pretense of aiding my grooming, and purr as she said: "You haven't the faintest fucking idea how to use it, do you?"

My ears flattened and I shot her a little sideways glare. I sometimes think there is something very unfeline about Dot.

"It's working," I heard Cinnamon mumble around the key.

We all looked. The beautiful Savannah cat was standing with her head held high, advancing slowly toward the water. As she went, the air appeared to part before her, creating a corridor with translucent walls. The effect was eerie; I had the sense that reality itself was being sliced open.

I stood behind Cinnamon and peered over her shoulder. The view directly before her was quite different from what we'd seen before. Here the island was not thirty body-lengths of thin, creaking ice away, but perhaps only eight or nine body-lengths distant from our paws, and surrounded by thick white ice.

I took a step to the left, and saw the old view of the pond; a step to the right, and perceived the same. Only directly in front of Cinnamon did the strange corridor, and its alternative version of our world, appear.

"Well done, Cinnamon," I said. I even managed a choked little purr. Gods damn it, I wish I'd known it would be that easy. Dot, I could tell, was smirking behind me; I could *feel* the schadenfreude radiating from her like a wave of sarcastic heat.

I swallowed my jealousy, and took a deep, cleansing, rib-heaving breath—which of course made my shoulder twinge. "Lead on," I told Cinnamon. "We'll follow."

With care Cinnamon, still holding her head—and the talisman—high, stepped onto the ice. It creaked beneath her substantial weight, but showed no signs of cracking. When she walked on, she left a large paw-print behind in the powdering of snow, which I took great care to step in exactly. I wasn't sure how picky the key would be about the dimensions of the path, and I had no desire to experiment. Cinnamon moved on, as did I, and I heard fainter creaks behind me as the others fell into line. She had to walk around a black branch poking above the ice once, and around half-submerged rocks twice, but the key bent the path to accommodate her, and the island remained in view.

A shadow moved beneath the ice, and I paused to observe it; when did a cat not stop to look at a fish? It certainly seemed fishlike, as it slid tantalizingly beneath the frozen surface. It also appeared to be growing in size...or, perhaps, getting nearer. Tail lashing with sudden unease, I lowered my head, putting my nose almost on the ice in a vain attempt to see beneath it.

"Go on, then, Spice," Dot grumbled behind me, but I didn't

answer: I was too shocked. In mere seconds the shadow, which had been the size of my paw, was now nearly the size of me altogether. Whatever it was, it was rushing the ice!

"Go!" I snapped at Cinnamon. The Savannah, bless her, never hesitated. In two swift jumps she'd made it to the shore of the little island. I followed suit with a mighty leap of my own. Even as I was in midair, I could hear Dot's rapid breathing behind me. I landed on the island and turned at once, to face whatever might be coming.

There was no monster emerging from hidden depths—yet. But there was Libby, as frozen as the river itself, staring down at the black shadow that rose to swallow him.

Crack! The ice heaved sickeningly, thrusting upwards... then slowly sank back into place. Water started seeping from new cracks in the surface, and the whole area sagged a little more than before. One more good hit, and it would shatter altogether.

"Libby!" I called. "Quickly!"

"It's coming!" he squalled, legs braced, ears flattened with terror.

He was right. Even from where I was, I could see the shadow expanding, as the creature raced toward us once more. I kept my eyes upon the obscure shape as I careened onto the ice, slipping and sliding my way around the cracked, sinking area. It was the size of my head...the size of my body...

I seized the scruff of Libby's neck roughly, not caring for my teeth, and hauled him after me like an oversized kitten. If he'd been any larger, I wouldn't have been able to budge him, he was that petrified by fear. My claws scraped across the ice as I pulled him after me; with every painful step I lost traction.

Crack! The ice thrust upward once more, and this time it

did break. Luckily, the impact actually threw us backwards, nearly all the way to the island's narrow shore. I released Libby and we scrabbled onto the sand, before turning to gape at the monstrosity that had shattered the ice.

It was an enormous, carp-like fish, twice as big as any of us, with alabaster scales edged in gold. That sounds beautiful, but its eyes were a flat, dead yellow, and they glared at us as it writhed amidst the shards of ice. Angrily it snapped in our direction; its long, needle-sharp teeth appeared to go all the way down its deep red throat.

Finally, with a last frustrated *smack* of its tail, it disappeared beneath the water once more, returning to impossible depths that surely couldn't exist in this pond.

Libby huddled against me, shaking so hard it shivered my own bones. "Toto," he whispered, staring at the massive hole left in the ice, "I don't think we're in Kansas anymore."

"What does that mean?" Cinnamon wondered.

"It's from a movie…" Libby muttered. He swallowed hard and managed to sit up, still shaking. No sooner had he accomplished that, than he collapsed back into me—this time, to offer me a quick swipe of his cheek, and a grateful nuzzle under my chin. "Thanks, Spice."

"You're lucky you're little," I teased him. I groomed his ear for a moment, steadying him with long, soothing licks, until he no longer trembled. That was just long enough for *me* to start shaking, not so much from adrenaline—I'd been in worse scrapes just yesterday—but from the state of my injured shoulder. I shouldn't have put so much weight upon it. Gingerly I pressed my paw to the sand, and could not suppress a hiss as pain lanced all the way from the base of my neck to the tips of my toes.

"Maybe you should have gone to the vet after all," Cinnamon said, sniffing dubiously at my barely-scabbed shoulder.

If I could have put my weight on that leg, I would've whacked her on the nose. Suggesting a cat willingly go to the vet! I mean, *really.* "I just need to rest," I said stiffly.

"Bullshit," said Dot cheerfully. "You can barely walk. Stay here, and keep the key. *We'll* explore the island."

"But...but..." I couldn't find the words I needed, to sound properly authoritative. *But this is MY string,* the kitten within me yowled. *You can't take it away from me!*

"Fine," I snapped, succumbing to hated reason. "Give me the damn key. And hurry up. And be *careful.*"

Cinnamon nosed the key over, sliding it across the sand to rest before my paws. I ignored it utterly, gazing out over the pond as if I'd spotted something interesting there. Dot, at last managing to heed basic cat etiquette, took my dismissal for what it was. She quietly led the others away, through the ring of bare-branched bushes that surrounded the island's interior. They were out of sight soon enough—especially in the fog that still hovered, oblivious to the sun's valiant efforts—but I could hear them crunching and conversing for some time.

As soon as they'd left, bone-deep lassitude nearly overwhelmed me. Nothing in this world sounded better than stretching out and taking a little cat nap. After all, I'd hardly slept; and it had been nearly a full day since I'd last ventured in the dreamworld. It would be good to stretch and race and leap without this throbbing, burning pain in my shoulder; good to chase small, squeaking shadows in the sunset city, or curl up in front of a friendly fire and a bowl of fat cream in Ulthar. I might even track down that rascal Solar again, so he could regale me with more stories of stolen lifetimes in the dreamlands… But no. The others were counting on me to keep watch, and protect the key. I dared not even rest my eyes.

The shadows lengthened as I waited, wondering what could be taking so long. The thin, brittle branches of the scrub grew too, rising upward, transforming into a dark and silent forest. Eventually, I got to my feet and ventured further inland, to find my friends.

The aroma of pine lay heavy; I inhaled the scent gladly as I wandered, enjoying as I never had before the silence of the hidden forest, its deep hollows and secret, shadowy places. A quiet descended upon my mind. Rather than move on to the sunset city or Ulthar or anywhere else in the dreamlands, I thought I might tarry here awhile, and rest in a bed of pine needles, which had accumulated in enormous drifts beneath their mother pines, untouched by the wind in this still wood.

I was just settling into my nest, purring a drowsy song—when it occurred to me that it was a good thing I hadn't gone to sleep while on guard duty. I opened my eyes, my "dream eyes" at least. I was in the dark pine forest between worlds. How had I gotten here? Surely the adventure was over and I was back at home, snuggled into a warm pile of blankets. I wouldn't have fallen asleep alone, and unprotected, on that island's barren shore…

I began to wake, my mind stubbornly drawing my exhausted body from the beguiling dreamlands. In that long, long second during which my soul hovered between worlds, the pine needle nest became much less comfortable. It began to prick, and to squeeze. It began to feel as hard against my side as old, cold bone.

With a mighty effort I opened my eyes—and beheld nothing but white. White fog was everywhere, opaque as cotton fluff. Yet something gripped me hard, crushing me against the sand, tightening cruel claws over my ribs. Bewildered, I struggled against an invisible enemy, one that hid in the mists and strangled me from behind. I could barely breathe from the pressure. Floating black dots crowded my vision, and I wondered: how much more could this poor body take?

Then I saw a *particular* spot in front of my eyes, one larger and differently-shaped from the others. I stretched my paw out a few millimeters, and hooked a claw over the key talisman's leather ring. Something like electricity shot down my spine, and whatever was squeezing me spasmed, as if in pain. Its grip slackened slightly. In an instant I violently wiggled myself free, scooped up the talisman (and a mouthful of sand), and wheeled to face my unseen opponent.

There was nothing there.

I blinked in shock for a moment or two, and looked dumbly about myself, with the naivete of a newborn kitten. Then I recovered my senses, blinked, and re-focused my eyes in that special way, to See That Which Cannot Be Seen.

When I saw it, ice gripped my guts, gnawing all the way down to the base of my spine. My tail puffed, the hair stood all along my back, and I hissed even as I scrambled madly backwards.

Eyes!

The mist was full of floating, disembodied eyes. Hundreds of white, blank, staring orbs. Following me. Watching me.

A claw scraped down my back. I yowled and turned what was almost a complete somersault, but my shoulder betrayed me, and I landed badly in an awkward crouch. From there, I craned my head back, watching the mist gather itself above me. It seemed to be thickening into an increasingly solid shape. I looked up…and up…at what the fog was assembling from itself.

It was a giant, bony hand, twice as tall as any human, with nasty, sharp talons at the end of six lengthy fingers. And it was coming straight at me.

Injured shoulder or not, it was time to go. I leapt away, talisman carried tightly between my teeth, and fled toward the middle of the island. The hand followed me—I could see its enormous shadow faintly outlined just ahead of my own. I was directly beneath the palm. It had only to bring its hand down to squash me flat, the way you'd squash an ant…

The shadow wavered across the ground. Following my instincts, I dodged sharply right, and just in time, for the hand collided with earth only a second later. The *thud* must have been audible to any humans on the shore. Sand flew in a stinging spray, half-blinding me, but I dared not stop.

At least I'd gotten the others' attention, for while I blinked and stumbled onward, I sensed—more than saw—three warm furry bodies near me.

"Time to go!" I yelled, and promptly doubled on my own tracks, running for all I was worth. I could just see well enough now to avoid the dark forms of bushes, though their thorn-like branches tore at my face and flanks as I dashed heedlessly past. I heard another thud, and a squeal from Libby, but even then I could not halt.

We were upon the island's narrow beach. The other shore seemed impossibly distant, at least thirty body-lengths of dark, questionable ice away. I stared dumbfounded, still running, before the solution occurred to me—of course, the way needed to be opened. Luckily, I still held the nasty key in my mouth. From the beach I leapt toward the ice.

I was descending toward that thin, translucent glaze upon

the waters, in whose frigid depths I was surely about to drown. Then, the key kicked in. I landed on thick white ice, and saw directly in front of me the safe path to the near shore. Yet the ice wobbled sickeningly as I slipped and slid across, for it had broken into several pieces after the fish's attack.

Two-thirds of the way across, I at last dared to check behind myself, to See That Which Cannot Be Seen. The giant hand had vanished utterly. All that remained were thick mists…and the hundreds of blind, staring, hovering eyes within. As I looked, a new form began to gather in the fog. Long rows of solid white columns appeared, with sharp points on their ends, arranged tightly together in a peculiar order. It took a moment for me to recognize what they represented: an enormous, disembodied mouth, stuffed to the brim with dozens of jagged teeth.

The teeth clacked in my direction, and bared themselves, all while the many eyes turned their blank orbs upon me. Then, slowly, they all began to dissolve. The mist drifted away, toward the center of the island, and even when I looked for That Which Cannot Be Seen, I could see—nothing.

The others had also paused upon the ice, and watched the creature's departure with fur raised and tails bristling. I was glad to see Libby was with us. I was really afraid he'd been killed.

"Everyone all right?" I asked.

I glimpsed motion in the corner of my eye, and leapt sideways—without a moment to spare. The ice heaved under our feet, sending us sliding, and the great white fish jumped from the dark hole it had made, leaving the water entirely. For a moment, the beast appeared to hang in the air, its gold-edged scales glimmering in the weak winter sunlight. Then it slammed into the the ice a mere tails-width from my feet, its massive, toothy jaws snapping at my paws.

I could have clawed it, but all claws were employed in scrambling away from that vicious mouth, on a slick sheet of ice that steadily tilted more and more towards the monstrous, heavy fish. It writhed and twisted after me, pursuing me even as I struggled madly to escape.

It was fortunate that Dot, the consummate hunter, kept her head. Circling around me, she flung herself upon the fish's abdomen, and raked its massive stomach nearly open. The fish twisted toward her, jaws gaping, but she dodged its lunge neatly, and leapt to a less shattered patch of ice. There she sat coolly, one paw raised and ready, as if to say, "You want some more?"

Blood oozed freely from the scratches she'd left, pooling on the ice. The carp at last appeared to surrender. It wiggled and flopped back into its hole, sliding tail-first into the mysterious depths. For a moment it lingered, its head just above the surface, still glaring at us. You could almost hear the little fishy gears grinding in its head—could it make a second attempt?

"Run," I was about to calmly suggest to the group (perhaps not so calmly). But before I could speak, the fish's protruding eyes bulged even further. It happened almost too fast to see, but I just glimpsed a green, clawed hand rise, dripping, from the water, to seize the massive fish by its flapping gill. The huge fish thrashed and fought the entire way, but it was dragged down, down, down, with a certain horrible inevitability. In no more than a breath or two, there was nothing left but a string of slowly popping bubbles.

I don't know what possesses me to do these things. Before any rational thought could rein me in, I was crouched upon the edge of the hole, peering down to see what had taken the fish. The waters were dark, but I could just make out vague movements far below. These coalesced into a certain silhouette, decidedly un-fish-like in its nature. I caught a golden gleam—yellow eyes that glowed, like lamps, amidst the black depths. Their shine turned my way, and for a long moment, I stared down at it, and it stared up at me. I blinked first, and backed away from the edge. I didn't care to wait and see what conclusion the Deep One might come to.

* * *

The next thing I remember, I was up the hill and in some strange human's backyard, quite a distance from that icy bank. I was lying down and Dot was giving my shoulder a good licking, while Cinnamon purred into my ear, and Libby scolded me.

"...should have stayed home! I mean, really!"

"What happened?" I murmured. I tried to stir, but Dot put a firm paw upon me and continued her vigorous ministrations.

"You don't remember?"

"She's in shock," said Cinnamon succinctly, in between throaty, soothing purrs. "She needs help."

Dot paused her licking, apparently in sudden doubt. "Are you dying?" she wanted to know. The subtext being, "If you're dying, I'll stop this waste of good saliva." It wasn't bad manners: we cats don't share the same fear of mortality as humanity, largely because we've already died before, and remember doing it.

So I checked in with my body to discover whether I was,

indeed, dying. I was in agony, and exhausted, and in shock, as Cinnamon had suggested. But I didn't sense that inner unraveling, the sensation of gradually slipping away, that usually marks death.

"Not if I get in the warm," I muttered. "And rest. And…" I heaved a sigh. "Maybe go to the damn vet."

"Can you get home, do you think?" Dot wanted to know.

"If I sleep first." I shivered—I was still quite wet, from all the fish's wild splashing—and curled up, with an effort. I even managed to draw my tail over my cold nose. "Can you get a little closer?"

So that was what happened. For the rest of the day I laid quite still behind a hedge, drifting from this world to the dreamlands and back. My friends took turns sleeping beside me, to keep me warm, and to watch over my exhausted naps.

At last, by evening, I felt well enough to travel. Dot and Libby escorted me home, taking long ways and dead ends and narrow, pissy alleys all over town, to avoid any trouble, for I wasn't certain yet I could climb a tree. But I rested as we went, and drank a little water, and even swallowed the head of a mouse, kindly offered by a handsome tuxedo called Onyx, with whom I was slightly acquainted.

By sunset, I was home, approaching the house from my large, forested backyard. As we came out from under the trees, though, I sat heavily, and stared in disbelief.

There were three night-gaunts perched upon my roof.

We cats glared at the night-gaunts, from the (relatively) safe shadows of the snow-laden trees. The night-gaunts, having no eyes, could not reciprocate—but their eerie, misshapen heads swiveled in our direction.

So focused was I on the night-gaunts, I almost didn't catch

the subtle sounds emerging from the house. When I did, though, I pointed my ears toward the attic, and leaned forward in concentration.

Was that…chanting?

My baby howled abruptly, screaming in terror. I didn't stop to think. No injury or exhaustion or night-gaunt could have held me then. I limped toward the house, moving as fast as I could, and dove through the cat-flap.

I saw later the bloody footprints I left on the carpet, but at the moment I was conscious of nothing but the shrieks of my baby. Up the stairs I darted, to peer around the door of his room. I would take them by surprise, whoever they were. I would leap upon their chests, knock them down, and scratch their eyes out. See if I wouldn't!

There was just one problem: nobody was there. That is, nobody except my baby, standing up in his crib and howling as if a thousand demons had come to devour him. I looked to See That Which Cannot Be Seen—and perceived nothing but a full diaper and a snotty nose. Neither of which are, frankly, particularly supernatural.

Puzzled, I sat down in the doorway. This was a mistake, as only a second later Morwen nearly ran me over. She also had come running—all right, waddling—in response to my baby's shrieks.

It's ok, darling, mama's here, I understood her to say, as she lifted him out of the crib and cradled him in her arms. My presence must have registered belatedly, for once the baby had quieted, she turned sharply toward the door, her eyes wide, her mouth a silent O.

Pumpkin Spice! What happened to you?!

"Oh, you know," I said, demurely. "This, that, and the other.

Trying to save the town, darling, that's all."

You naughty cat! She plopped my baby down in his crib again, prompting fresh wails from him, which she now ignored. Kneeling before me, she probed my injuries with gentle fingers, and soothed the fur along my ears. I purred, rather feebly, I admit, at her ministrations.

You awful kitten, I was so worried about you!

"And I you," I responded, rubbing my cheek against the side of her hand. I caught an interesting whiff of scent as I did, something I hadn't smelled in a long time: incense. Dragon's blood, to be precise.

You come with me, I'm taking you to the vet right now!

I suddenly understood why not one, not two, but *three* nightgaunts were resting upon our rooftop. I could also make a guess as to the source of the chanting, and even why Morwen had been absent from my baby's room. Put all these facts together, and the conclusion left me purring, even as Morwen hauled me bodily to the dreaded plastic cat carrier.

My witch was practicing again!

7

Maddening

The next day I spent almost entirely in the dreamlands. Trapped in a tiny overflow cage in the stuffy vet's office—for "observation"—there was little else to do. The first country I visited was Ulthar, and though cats of all sizes, shapes, and colors crowded upon the wide hearths of the Arched Back Inn, I could not spot Solar's tawny fur among them. So I slipped away into the sunset city, taking an interdimensional shortcut through the silent forest, which—now that I was no longer in shock—remained as eerie and discomforting as usual.

But the sunset city was what it always was, and I was free to ignore the shadows of unknown cats, and to sprawl lazily upon warm, sunny flagstones in the grass-choked streets. Intriguing little shadows hopped and squeaked nearby, and I thought about rising to catch them—and then again, perhaps not. It was a beautiful early evening, there where it's always early evening, and it became even better when I heard a familiar purr above me.

"May I?"

"Sure," I said, though somewhat surprised. I rolled over, so that Tilly could join me. She was in her dreamlands form, young and beautiful, with velvety black fur and a white star upon her chest. No mangy fur or broken tail or cataracts for her here. With a sigh she flopped down, stretching full-length upon the smooth stone, and I snuggled my back into the warmth of her.

We dozed like that for some time, with no movement but the occasional flick of an ear. At last Tilly rolled over and sat up. Putting one paw on my face to hold me still, as if I were a mere kitten, she bent down to lick my ear into shape.

"You look like hell," she observed.

From my prone position I tried to look at myself. "I thought I looked normal."

"Underneath the dream-form, I mean. Your chi is just a mess."

"I'm at the vet's," I told her drowsily. The combination of it all—the sun, the hot stone, the maternal grooming—was extremely pleasant. I began to feel I was a kitten, after all. Old, simple memories emerged, of blind groping towards the soft warmth of Mother, and of seizing a nipple to enjoy spurts of hot, sweet milk. "I got pretty torn up."

"So? What happened?" Tilly wanted to know.

Sleepily, I related all that had passed since our last encounter. The peculiar fight I'd observed between my humans, my visit to the temple of visions, the albino ghoul, the mist monster he'd led us to, the Deep Ones we encountered at every turn—at least, every turn with water in it. When I'd finished, Tilly ceased her slow grooming, though her paw remained pressed into my cheek, so that I could not move.

Just as I was about to try and sit up anyway, she spoke. "This seems much more complicated, and serious, than I'd realized. That incident with the car…"

I *mrrowed* in soft affirmation. She went on: "Yet you seem to be doing a decent job of handling it. I've been worried about leaving Kingsport in this time of crisis, though at my advanced age it seems inevitable. I'm a little less bothered, now, since you seem to have emerged as a leader amongst the youngsters."

At six years old I was hardly a youngster, but I wasn't going to argue away praise—that would be downright uncat-like. "Thank you," I purred. "But…what about…?"

"The King?" she guessed, when I was unwilling to finish my query. "Hah! Toms. And that one in particular. Oh, a King is all well and good to keep social order amongst the cats, and to make sure plenty of kittens are born. But no King *I've* ever known trapped and questioned a ghoul. Even—" here she paused mischievously—"if it was mostly by accident."

Accident or no, I was purring so hard I'm sure it could be heard three blocks in every direction.

"Or made it to the haunted island in the middle of the pond," she went on. "Speaking of which—you said the ghoul told you they'd made a deal with that thing?"

"That's what he said."

"Hmm." She sounded quite disbelieving.

I raised my head—with difficulty, as she was still holding me down. Even now she didn't move her paw off my face. "You don't think so?"

"I've been alive a long time, and never heard a peep from that island. Oh, you can't *get* there, and you *know* something's there, of course, but…"

"It never leaves?"

She looked at me. "Don't you think you would've noticed it before?"

I considered. Damn it, Tilly was likely right. Also, now that I thought about it, the creature hadn't been interested in pursuing us or even *really* in killing us—because it could have, easily. It had just wanted us to leave. Did that square with whatever aggressive enchantment was shaking Kingsport loose from its foundings? No, blast it, it did not.

"That son of a bitch lied to me!" I exclaimed.

Tilly chuckled. "Probably."

"He was just trying to get us killed!"

"You bet."

With a groan I slumped back onto the flagstone. Tilly patted my cheek sympathetically.

"Listen, Spice," she said. "I have to go—Violet will be home soon, and there are things I need to take care of before she gets back. Take this. You need it more than I do."

Holding me firmly down, she bent forward and touched noses with me. The touch shocked me slightly, and I blinked.

In that blink, Tilly was gone. She'd already returned to the material world.

My nose still stung from the static. I wrinkled it, and sneezed. With the sneeze—as if I'd broken a barrier—a wave of heat surged through my body. It was so distinct an impression, and so different from anything I'd ever experienced, that I found myself on my feet, shuddering from head to toe. Gradually the warmth ebbed away, though it lingered as a pleasant kind of afterburn, and I stopped my mad shivering.

What had caused *that*? Had something happened to my body while I was in the dreamlands? Uneasily I considered awakening. Was it better to know? Or to sleep through whatever unpleasantness the vet might be inflicting?

My somewhat queasy meditations were interrupted by Libby, who charged around the corner with all the grace and composure of a dog.

"There you are!" he exclaimed, pouncing upon me and nearly knocking me over. At first I thought he was in the mood to play, or even to mate (Libby sometimes forgets I'm fixed), but a good sniff revealed the acrid stench of fear, and convinced me that his pupils were dilated with terror, not mischief.

"What's wrong, Libby?" I asked, pushing him off me, and pointedly grooming my ruffled chest fur.

"There are night-gaunts at my house!"

I looked at him sideways. "Libby, there were night-gaunts at your house before. You said so. And there were *three* at mine. Three! It's because—"

"But there are *seventeen!*"

I stopped what I'd been about to say, about Morwen resuming the craft. I'm afraid I rather gaped at him.

"Seventeen?" I echoed.

"Seventeen!"

I laid my ears against my head. "I was just speaking with Tilly. She's convinced me the albino ghoul lied to us."

I wouldn't have thought Libby's pupils could grow larger, but I would've been wrong. The twin black holes nearly swallowed the irises. "So the mist monster thing *doesn't* have anything to do with the night-gaunts, and the time shifts, and all the rest of it?"

My teeth ground together before I could admit, "No. Maybe not. I don't know." I added, after further grinding, "And…I'm sorry I put you all in danger to follow up on some stupid lead from a stupid ghoul." My ears flattened even further against my skull, and I dipped my head submissively. "I should've known he was lying."

Libby sat back and stared at me, seeming quite astonished. "Well, goodness, Spice, you're only feline, you know. And we've all been worried about what's happening in Kingsport, and we all agreed to go with you. It wasn't as if you could have *made* us go." He chuckled suddenly. "You know, the humans have a saying about herding cats."

"Oh? What do they say?"

"That it's impossible." Libby licked his nose in amusement. "And Mark and Clarence's friend Amy always says it about *them*, whenever she's trying to get them somewhere on time."

"That is funny." I pondered the wise saying while surreptitiously studying Libby. Bless him, he'd regained his composure in almost no time at all. The Devon Rex was a resilient little cat, for all his funny ways.

As for myself, I also felt much better. A little time in the dreamlands appeared to have done me wonders. And while the albino ghoul might have gotten the better of us, I still had faith in my vision in the divining pool of the lost temple. It proved the ghouls were involved in some way; I just had to figure out *how.*

I twisted round to lick a few back hairs into order, preparatory to testing Libby's recovery.

"I still think," I began rather cautiously, "that the ghouls are the key to solving this problem."

"You don't want to *talk* to one again, do you?" Libby asked at once, narrowing his enormous eyes.

"No." I dismissed the notion with a flick of my ear. "But we might consider *following* them, and observing them from a distance."

Libby's tail thrashed uneasily, and he shifted from paw to paw. "How *much* of a distance?"

"You know," someone interrupted, "there's always another option."

The black panther form of the King stalked around the corner. The hair along my spine bristled, and I fought the urge to arch my back. Even if you knew, for certain, that the material form of the King was merely that of a short-haired domestic, it's hard to shut down that part of your brain that shrieks, *Giant predator prowling this way!*

"Yes, sir?" Libby asked, crouching down low on the weed-choked flagstones, so that he was half-hidden by bobbing wildflowers. "What's that?"

"Leave," the panther suggested. He rested his enormous hindquarters on the road, giving us all a nice, clear look at his oversized genitalia.

By the stars, I missed the old king, Big Red. He hadn't been *classier*, exactly—big, swinging balls, and the personality to go with them, being a prime requisite of cat royalty. He'd been just, somehow, more likeable about it all. And he'd been my father, too, though fatherhood means comparatively little amongst us cats.

"Leave?" Libby queried, now three-quarters hidden behind the weeds.

"Leave," the panther affirmed, addressing me, as if I'd spoken. "Soon."

"What good would leaving do?" I asked. "You can't escape time!"

"The effects in Kingsport are purely local," said the King, eyes slitted sleepily. "I have it on good authority that these phenomena barely extend past the town's borders. Everything is quite normal, just a half-day's walk away."

"And is retreat your intention, then? Your Majesty?" I asked, endeavoring to keep as polite a tone as possible. I noted that my claws had unsheathed themselves; though the gesture was unconscious, I did not attempt to retract them.

"If necessary," the panther said languidly. "I am monitoring the situation closely. Should Kingsport prove temporarily unsafe, I'll form a court and take up residence in an abandoned barn just south of here, until the situation passes. You may join us, if you so desire."

I was surprised that the King had thought this far ahead, and also that he'd invited us—me, a fixed female, and Libby, a (theoretically) competing male. "Thank you," I said, although I immediately rather wished I hadn't. "We'll consider it."

"I'll want that key back before we leave," the King said. Then the panther rose gracefully, hindquarters swinging, and stalked past us without further ado. Perhaps he was off to spread the word of his proposed refugee court. I wondered if he'd already spoken to Dot. Surely he'd at least tried to track down Cinnamon, a prime specimen who'd just reached breeding age.

I also pondered, briefly, what had become of the key. I'd been far too groggy to keep track of the talisman after our battle with the giant fish, and no cat had mentioned it since.

"What do you think?" I asked Libby. "About the court?"

Libby, still flattened to the ground, shook his head, sending the tall-stemmed flowers around him quivering and shaking. "Not here!" he hissed. "We'll speak in the material realm."

"Then we'd better get back to it. Let's meet at twilight by Burying Hill. Tell Dot and Cinnamon if you see them, by chance."

"What, the graveyard? Again?!"

"We'll be more careful this time," I assured him, and woke myself up before he could argue further.

* * *

My body was still in the cramped overflow cage with its flimsy wire walls and omnipresent smell of piss. With difficulty, my face jammed against the door, I stretched as best as I could. I was feeling pretty good—better than I'd felt in ages, in fact. You'd never hear me admit to Morwen, though, that a *vet* could make me *well*.

There remained the question of how I intended to escape this place in time to visit Burying Hill by twilight. With care I managed to squirm a paw through the door and pat at the latch, but could achieve no leverage. Damn. I had no idea when Morwen intended to rescue me, and even when she had, past experience taught me she was bound to keep a close watch on my movements for some time afterwards. Besides, I'd already hurt her feelings once, running away after the wreck; I didn't want to send her into one of her pouts by repeating an apparent betrayal. Yet who could blame a cat for running away from the vet? With the right approach, I could probably make Morwen feel guilty for leaving her "poor baby" at the "mean ol' vet's" for such a lengthy period—and more guilt invariably meant more catnip treats. I caught myself purring at the very thought.

"What have you got to purr about?" a sour cat voice sounded from somewhere above. I ignored it. More difficult to block out were the whines and pleas from the canine prisoners around me, and the occasional scream that tore itself from a terrified rabbit. The cages were quite full at this time of year, what with humans travelling home for the holidays. The usual wall of stainless steel compartments had been completely occupied by the time I arrived; hence my placement in a spare cage shoved into a corner, where I was already accumulating neighbors as yet more animals poured in.

Still, in some ways we were the lucky ones, for other humans were busy turning their homes into animal deathtraps. One poor kitten had been brought in more dead than alive, having accidentally hung himself in a Christmas tree's lights. The doctor had revived him, but even without a vet's fancy equipment, I could tell that the pitiful little thing would never be the same. Better luck next lifetime.

And now, to add to all the noise, some sort of ruckus was taking place in the front office. I cocked my ear in that direction, only to wince at an incessant, high-pitched canine whine. Drunken slurring from a human raised my suspicions, and a quick sniff confirmed: the vet's office had been breached by the Bastard Pack.

They burst through the door of the back room like chaos incarnate: the owner staggering on every step and dragging on a chain his enormous mastiff, which yelped and cried with the earnestness of a newborn pup. They weren't supposed to be back here, I was sure, but that was explained by the human himself, in speech whose intent was shockingly clear to my ears:

I don't care if the vets are busy, you'll see him now, damn it!

Given his red eyes and the smell of his breath, I bet I understood him better than the poor, flustered female tech trying to usher him out.

The human, with surprising strength, wrapped his arms

around the hulking canine and heaved him onto an operating table. As my cage was on the floor, this put the dog a little above my line of sight, but I could hear him quite clearly as he thrashed and whined. "Ow, ow, it bites, it bites! Off! Off!" he called in his own language, of which, sadly, I understood more than a little. In previous lifetimes it had behooved me to learn the speech of canines; like our own (and unlike that of humans), it was based more on body language, scent, and the shared unconscious of the species than verbalization. There were a number of differences between our own methods of communication and that of canines, but I could generally comprehend what a dog said, and even make shift to respond in the same, if I wanted to.

While the vet tech and the owner argued, I pressed my face against the door of the cage, and said, as clearly as I could in the simple language of dogs, "What's wrong? What's on you?"

"It bites, it bites!" was the dog's only answer. By crouching down low and craning my eyes upward, I could just see the mastiff on the surgical table, gnawing frantically at a front leg that was already bloodied and torn.

...lost one dog already, and another killed in my own goddamn yard, and now this one here's gone crazy... The distraught, drunken dog owner's rant overpowered the meaning of the tech's soothing speech.

I summoned my powers, closed my eyes, and reopened them to See That Which Cannot Be Seen. Was I surprised to perceive a small yet loathsome creature of shadow, more mouth than body, with tentacles where there should be limbs, fastened upon the mastiff's leg by leech-like suckers? I was not. But I was a little taken aback at the darkness that hovered around his owner. It was a black fog, save where small stabs of red could be glimpsed: crimson lightning in a thunderstorm from hell. I noted that with each flash of red the drunkard's voice pitched a little higher, and a little louder. He was working himself into a frenzy. Meanwhile, his dog whimpered and thrashed, trying to bite at a creature his teeth could not physically meet. It must have been maddening.

"I will help you," I told the dog, with my stilted pidgin. His floppy ear perked, and he spared a second to roll his wide eyes my way, searching the cages for whoever had spoken. "Down here!" I called, and his eyes fell upon me.

Deeply as I dislike dogs, as a Maine Coon (well, half, anyway), they have a trifle more respect for me than for your average cat. Besides, this dog was desperate. He did not waste time.

"How?" he wanted to know. Before I could answer, though, he yipped in pain and fell back upon his leg, gnawing busily at his own flesh. All the while, the blackness surrounding his master grew thicker.

"Come down here, break the door, get me out. I will help you," I told him. When he did not respond, I barked a command: "Quick! Do it now! NOW!"

The great sin of dogs is obedience. The huge mastiff rolled off the table. Though he landed on the injured leg with a yelp, he did not hesitate: he charged my cage full force.

WHAM! The thin walls of my collapsible cage shuddered under the impact. The noise became truly deafening as every animal in the room cried out—with fear or with excitement, it scarcely mattered. Both the drunkard and the tech put their hands over their ears.

I sighed. "Over here!" I said. "Hit the door." The dog shook his head, clearly a little stunned by the din. "Put your shoulder into it!" I snapped. "Quick, before they stop you! NOW!"

Again the Mastiff charged, this time directly at the door, and threw his hefty shoulder into it. The latch could not withstand his weight, and the door flew violently open; had I not been crouched at the back, I would have received a face-full of cage. I leapt to the floor and was immediately drooled upon by the foamy-mouthed mastiff, who glared at me with bloodshot eyes.

"Fix it!" he said. He probably meant to say it fiercely, but the pitiful whine that erupted, and the way he was trembling from tail to snout, undermined the implicit threat.

In any case I was not looking at him but at the humans in the room. The horror-struck tech had rushed around the table and was a mere tail-length from the mastiff, her hand outstretched to catch his spiked collar. The drunk owner was also veering around the table from the other side; he too, was hurrying, and he too, had his hands raised, but he was coming at the vet tech, not at the dog, and the cloud around him was blacker than sin...

The tech was closer to me. I sprang at her, all claws unsheathed, and scratched wildly at her legs. She shrieked and retreated, though not much damaged—I was not trying for blood, but for fright. Meanwhile, the dog's owner had stumbled right past his animal and was still coming for the tech. He started to swing big, horny fists.

Get your damn hands off my damn dog! The words burst forth with a howl that was not fully human. The hair on my back shivered upright as the darkness surrounding him shrieked in chorus with his words. Into his open, sneering mouth the black fog poured, and into his ears, and into his eyes. I could no longer see the man's face: I was beginning to wonder if there was any man left to see.

"Get your human out!" I demanded of the mastiff. He looked

up from his incessant chewing, and saw his master charging the bewildered woman. I'll give him this much credit—the dog didn't hesitate. Lunging forward, he seized a solid mouthful of faded jeans—and perhaps of his buttocks, too—and hauled backwards.

Had that mastiff been any other breed, it might never have worked. But while the owner cursed and twisted round to swat at his muzzle, the mastiff dragged him steadily, implacably, back. The drunk, wobbly-legged human proved no match for his massive animal, and he was pulled unceremoniously from the back room and into the hall. Another vet opened the door of an examination room and peered out, just as the receptionist hurried in from the lobby.

The mastiff released the man and limped around to face him, barking and whining. The man looked from the people staring at him, to the dog whimpering in front of him, and sighed. I watched closely, fascinated by the oily, smoke-like substance that poured forth from his nose and mouth, along with that sigh. The dark substance still clung to his skin, half-obscuring his face, but it was no longer shot through with bloody crimson crackles.

Yeah, fuck these people, let's get out of here, the man mumble-sneered. He managed to turn himself around and careen into a Fire Exit, which he opened without appearing to notice the ear-splitting alarm. The mastiff limped after him, and I took this opportunity to trot at the dog's heels, as if I'd been with them all along.

They got as far as the corner before the man sat down on the curb. Putting his head in his hands, he began to weep, noisily and apparently without noticing the nervous looks and sideways glances of passerby. The mastiff was the epitome of a fine canine specimen; despite the shadowy creature still suckling on its leg, he bravely shuffled over to his owner, and laid his slobbery-jawed head on the human's shoulder, drooling all over his shirt in the process. His tail beat the snow-dusted pavement with a reassuring *thwap, thwap.* The man burst into fresh tears and laid his head against the dog's own, reaching up one shaking hand to caress the suffering animal's skull.

*I'm so sorry, boy...*the man moaned. I continued to be astonished how clearly I understood him, who was so obviously a dog person. Perhaps he'd been educated by a cat when he was young. *I'm so sorry...first Billy's missing, and Mo gets killed, and now you're hurting and I can't even get you to the goddamn vet...*

Oh! Right! This, at least, was a problem I could solve. I practically had to lay my claws across the mastiff's flank before I could draw his attention, but at last the dog's eyes shifted my way, though his head remained firmly pressed to his master's shoulder.

"Hold still," I ordered the dog. *Thwap* went his tail in agreement.

Luckily, the affected foreleg was the one closest to me. I crouched low in an attempt not to draw the unstable human's notice, and focused my gaze to See That Which Cannot Be Seen.

The ugly little beast, with its razor-toothed suckers and tightly-wrapped tentacles, was still oozing and pulsating around the dog's leg. If anything, it appeared to have grown bigger, even in that brief interim. Impulsively I unsheathed my claws...and then, deliberately, let them subside. Where a dog's teeth wouldn't work, a cat's claws wouldn't do either. There are Things Which Cannot Be Seen that are primarily material—such as ghouls—and then there are those that aren't.

This was evidently one of the latter.

I settled even lower, pressing my stomach to the frozen pavement. The creature rolled a triple-pupiled eye in my direction. Its cheeks—I suppose they were cheeks—fluttered yet faster, as if determined to finish the dog before I could finish it. It must have hurt, because even in the process of comforting his master, the mastiff could not restrain a long-drawn whine.

I patted my paws in the little drifts of dirty snow, scratching here and there a Mark with a claw. It was not a full circle, but a small assembly of signs that should protect and empower me. The being watched me with two of its eyes now, its body pulsating even quicker. An open sucker on its back began to twitch and shudder, gnashing the pointed teeth clustered around its rim.

I took a very, very deep breath. Prepared equally to spring and to flee, I launched into the same incantation I'd tried on the night-gaunt:

"Iaaaaahhhhhhoooooooorrrrroooooooooowwyeeeooooooowwwwy-eeow!"

The human startled upright, swearing and knocking his dog's head off his shoulder. He nearly fell onto his back trying to see what had made that sound. The shadowy entity on the dog's leg blanched—visibly blanched—and shivered violently. But it did not disappear.

The human was getting to his feet, as best as he could in his condition and on the slippery pavement. Fully expecting a boot to the head any moment, I looked at the mastiff. He, for his part, looked at his leg, and then at me, and growled. His teeth were stained nearly black, and were easily twice or even three times the size of my own.

"I will fix it!" I said at once. "But we need to—" Here I stopped: I didn't know the dog words for 'force the creature into the material realm.' Metaphysics had rarely been a feature of my previous conversations with canines.

Ah, there it was, the expected *Go on, get outta here!* and vicious kick at my ribs. Fortunately the kick was aimed poorly, and I didn't even bother to dodge. The human was now so off balance he stumbled into the street. It would be a few moments before he could work up the balance to kick again, or find something to throw.

Meanwhile, the dog's growls intensified. Laboriously, the mastiff climbed to three of his feet.

"I will heal it!" I hastily assured him, switching tactics.

"Then do it!" the dog snarled, limping forward. Towering overhead, he thrust the afflicted leg at me.

It wasn't easy to focus in that fashion, with the foam from the mastiff's muzzle dripping onto my skull, and his growl rumbling continuously in the background, punctuated only by his master's swearing. Yet I examined the leg and the nasty thing on it. It occurred to me that, insomuch as we could not bite the hideous little parasite, said parasite could not stop *me* from reaching the wound.

With a shudder I buried my face in the being's insubstantial mass, and delicately licked the bleeding tears all along the mastiff's forelimb. I could feel the parasite's presence as a cobwebby, shuddering sensation in my whiskers, but that was all. And while I groomed away the blood, I purred an old cat song, one I'd used before to tranquilize prey.

The soothing sounds and touch worked their small magics. The bleeding slowed, just as I'd willed it, and so did the mastiff's panting. When I at last jerked my head away, licking my lips in distaste, the dog gingerly put his paw to the pavement.

"It still hurts," he told me. "I can still feel it biting me. But it's better." He glanced from the leg to me, the many furry folds of his face even more mournful than before. "You can't fix it? You can't get it off?" He paused. "I'll die, won't I?"

My heart, such as it is, melted.

"I can fix it," I admitted to the dog. "But I need help. Need time. Meet me later?"

"When?"

"Twilight. By the crossroads near Burying Hill." I told it crisply. "You know it? You will come?"

The dog looked over at his master, who was hopping around on one foot trying to get his boot off. Presumably, he'd found nothing else to hurl at me. "I'll come," he said, and heaved a sigh. "But you better be there, cat. Or else."

It was an empty threat, and we both knew it. Though the creature was small, it was busily devouring the dog's life-force, not to mention driving the mastiff to near-madness. By twilight he would be in no shape to chase me, let alone kill me.

"I will," I said.

An old, smelly boot sailed in my direction. Luckily, the master's aim was no better the second time. I calmly watched the boot fly overhead and land in the brittle, frosted grass next to me.

A mother with an over-dressed baby glared at the drunkard from two storefronts over, shouted something, and slammed her way into the shop. I hadn't understood a word, but my guess was it had been something like, *That's it, I'm calling the cops!*

"You'd better get him out of here," I told the dog.

The dog growled under his breath and went to collect his errant master. Meanwhile, I slunk under a parked car, before the mastiff could change his mind. Happily, I discovered that there was a line of parked cars all the way back up the street: in other words, a nice little covered walkway for any cat who desired to travel unseen. As much as I didn't want to go anywhere near the vet clinic, this road was the fastest way to the graveyard and—rather more importantly—to Dot's house.

I did cross the street before I dared to pass the clinic, finding new shelter behind a thick hedge of holly. Peering between the prickly leaves, I checked to see whether the vets had begun the search for me yet.

As I watched, a battered old car, with exhaust pouring from its rear, pulled into the vet's tiny parking lot. An old woman with short-cut, salt-and-pepper hair emerged, carrying something in a purple blanket. She was evidently crying, and perhaps that made her careless, for a tail flopped out of the soft, fuzzy folds, to dangle lifelessly by the old woman's side.

I did not recognize the human, but I knew that battered tabby tail, with its broken, cock-eyed tip. Cold gripped my guts, a wave of ice that had nothing to do with the frigid winter weather. I sat up and bowed my head, honoring the passing of our elder.

For a long moment, I paused there, and pondered Tilly's conversation with me anew. I understood now what she'd meant, when she'd said she had "things to take care of" before Violet returned home—I, too, wished to spare my human the memory of my passing. I've never understood the penchant humans have for deathbeds surrounded by loved ones. Far, far better to slip away and be alone, when one at last experiences the ebbing sensation of imminent death.

The "shock" I'd experienced when Tilly had touched noses with me, and the curious praise she'd bestowed upon me, could be interpreted as a passing of the torch. She'd offered me what was left of her life-essence, so that I could accomplish the task of protecting Kingsport. Her body had grown old, after all, and she'd said herself she didn't want it to last past Christmas. Yet it was chilling to realize that I was the unwitting instrument of her demise, as well as the cause of an old human's grief.

I, too, grieved. True, it was quite likely I'd see Tilly again someday. But when, and how, and would we remember each other? We cats might retain our memories from lifetime to lifetime (although imperfectly), but we claim little control over our reincarnations. Upon death, each cat enters what we call the Lair, a place of darkness and rest, but also of confusion and loss. You might emerge from the Lair in two Earth days, or in two hundred years. You might recall the events of five lifetimes ago with crystal clarity, or you might blink at a kitten you birthed weeks before. Some, like Solar, found their way to the dreamlands; others, like myself, were repeatedly reborn in the same location. Worse, there was a chance one could be lured from the Lair in another form, and not be reborn as a cat at all.

Once, in Ulthar, I'd conversed with the prized pet cat of a powerful Tibetan lama, and he'd said some humans called that place the "bardo"—though their descriptions of it sounded rather peculiar to me.

At last, in the midst of my meditations, I saw the female vet tech open the door and peer into the parking lot. When she emerged, her arms wrapped around herself in a vain attempt to keep warm, and started checking under the cars, I knew the search for me had begun. I stole away with all secrecy, grateful for every hedge, fence, and car that obscured my not-insubstantial self from the world. It was already growing dark; there wasn't much time left to prepare for the coming exorcism.

8

Loathsome

I collected Dot from her house, a pristinely-preserved colonial that dated back to the 18th century, and which hadn't been altered in at least two of my lifetimes. Dot's human had money, but she also had taste and a good heart—hence her adoption of a particularly ugly little kitten from the Kingsport animal shelter. Among us, Dot was the only one who had traveled extensively in this lifetime; even when her human jetted off to London or Paris, Dot accompanied her in a comfortable carrier, and feasted on whatever tasty treats the five-star hotel chefs could concoct.

Yet despite this envious life of luxury, Dot was happiest when hunting. Hardly a day passed by that she didn't supplement her delicate diet with a mouse or vole or baby bird. Whole neighborhoods grew quiet when she padded through them. Birds ceased chirping and huddled onto their branches, while rodents held their breath and tried to quiet their tiny, pounding hearts—that is, if they didn't make a dash for distant holes, which is usually when they met Dot's claws.

I'm not a bad hunter myself, but even I bow before the master. Without Dot I never would have made it to the graveyard by twilight, carrying a stunned, plump chickadee carefully between my teeth.

It was an excruciating journey for us both, the chickadee and me. I salivated constantly, and with each little flutter or tremble longed to bite into the powdery fluff of its body, crunching down to the juicy bits. The bird, for its part, was badly wounded and only half-conscious, yet it must have known that death was imminent. I purred to it as I trotted, in the ancient cat way, soothing it somewhat with the repetitive rhythm.

We could smell the mastiff long before we saw him: the reek of blood and fear carried a long way on the wind. I wondered what else had smelled him. I wondered what else might be coming.

The dog had taken refuge from the coming night's bitter wind in a small stand of evergreens at the edge of a somewhat ramshackle yard, across the street from Burying Hill. Dot and I were careful to keep under dover as we progressed, since we didn't know what might be watching. We approached the evergreens from behind, and Dot chirped a little greeting as we went, lest we take the terrified dog by surprise.

"You came!" the mastiff said, as we slipped beneath low-hanging branches, and into the snow-free area of fallen needles sheltered by a triumvirate of old pines. The trees both protected and concealed us; I approved of the mastiff's thinking.

"Said I would," I told him in his own language, dropping the chickadee. Dot placed a quick paw on it before it could escape. It fluttered pitiably; I crouched beside it and increased the strength of my purr.

"Yes," the mastiff went on. He sounded confused. "But you're a *cat*."

"I'm here, too." Libby poked his head into the shelter—just his head. He was clearly shivering from head to toe, though whether with cold or with fear, that was difficult to tell. Certainly the great tan-and-black mastiff, with his drool-flecked jowls and potent stench of sickness and terror, was a heart-stopping sight on such a night. Or anytime, really.

"Please! Get it off," the mastiff begged, limping forward. I winced, for the leg was even worse than before, gnawed up and down by the dog's teeth, and bleeding great, steaming drops into the snow. When I focused to See That Which Cannot Be Seen, I could not restrain a hiss: the creature was twice the size of before. Again it rolled its loathsome, triple-pupiled eyes at me, and the razor-toothed sucker on its back rippled in warning. This time, however, I'd come prepared.

"Present the bird," I told Dot.

"I know how to do it," she grumbled, but pawed the panting chickadee toward the creature anyway. The bird quivered, beak opening and closing. One fragile leg was bent quite wrong. My tail twitched at the sight, for I am not the sort of cat to toy with my prey. I prefer to dispatch them at once, with a swift bite to the head, or a neck-snapping shake for bigger animals. But in this case it was necessary, and the little bird would soon take its well-deserved rest in the cosmic Lair—as Tilly had so recently. As, eventually, would we all.

Dot began the incantation, growling forth the words of the spell. I underlaid the incantations with a hearty, rib-shaking purr. Libby, bless him, crept fully into our evergreen cave and began to caterwaul over the top, as only a prowling tom can.

Out of the corner of my eye I registered a light turning on in the house behind us. We would have to be swift.

The shadowy parasite on the dog's leg visibly dimmed. It quivered and suckled faster, and the mastiff groaned in agony. Yet as the combined chant went on, the creature's outline grew blurred and vague, before it disappeared altogether. Even with our best vision, we cats could not actually observe the creature's transference; we sensed it passing by as a stench, a shock, a lingering sensation of cold.

The monster had vanished from the poor dog's leg—but the chickadee was filled with new, dark life. It thrashed furiously beneath Dot's steady paw, clacking its beak with a murderous rage never demonstrated by a chickadee before.

Dot did not delay. Her teeth met swiftly over the bird's head, and then she shook it for good measure—once, twice, thrice. The little body hung limp, having at last found peace.

With a grimace, Dot dropped it. "Don't eat it," she warned the mastiff, in her own attempt at the canine speech. She was rather better at it than me.

"What did you do?" the dog asked. He licked his leg tenderly, but his eyes were on the tiny puff of feathers in the snow.

Though I groaned internally, I did my best to translate the ceremony into dog. "It was not all here," I explained. "Some of it was somewhere else. Some other place. So you could not bite it."

"But it was biting me!"

"Yes, it hardly seems fair, does it?" Libby pondered.

"We brought it here, to this world," I plodded on. "Made it go inside the chickadee. The chickadee was between places anyway. Then, we killed the chickadee." I yawned, exhausted by my language efforts. "So the monster went."

"But don't eat it," repeated Dot.

"I mean," I prevaricated, "maybe it's ok, but…"

"Not worth the risk," said Dot flatly.

"No, certainly not." The mastiff paid good attention to his leg for a moment or two. I eased past him and peered out at the graveyard across the street. The sun had set properly now, and the blue light of twilight was fading into the rosy gray of a snowy winter sky—though it wasn't snowing yet. It might not be dark enough for the spy mission I'd intended.

"You know a lot about this thing," the mastiff said thoughtfully, after a lengthy interval of licking. "Does this happen often? I've never heard about it before."

"Oh, all the time," said Libby airily. "But usually to humans." He sniffed, and then promptly sneezed, having evidently gotten a snoot-full of pine. "They're so thick, too," he went on. "We tell them as much, and they ignore us. We even bring them sacrifices for the ceremony, and they screech at us about the 'dirty half-dead mouse' and being 'such cruel creatures.'"

"What'd he say?" the mastiff asked Dot—Libby had babbled in feline.

"Humans are stupid," said Dot, dismissing the entire species with a flick of her tail. "And usually, they're the victims."

"So why me?" the mastiff asked, in a plaintive tone that seemed odd from such a ferocious-looking beast. "Why now?"

"Because," I told him, "something is very, very wrong."

"There are monsters in the sewers," he said, his ears drooping even further than usual, and his tail creeping under his belly. "One pulled Billy down in. And something killed the big boss—that was Mo—in our own yard. He heard something, and went out through the dog door, and never came back." The mastiff whimpered at the memory. "We still don't know what got him."

"Many things come to Kingsport right now," I said.

"We think the ghouls are to blame," put in Libby. "They're up to some devilry with their allies the night-gaunts. We've come here to spy on them and see what they're doing."

"The ghouls?" The mastiff had doubtless grasped little of Libby's speech—but 'ghouls' was something he understood. "But the ghouls have left."

"They're gone?" I asked. I peered through the evergreens again, and squinted to See That Which Cannot Be Seen. Sure enough, I didn't see any ghouls…but then again, I couldn't see much of anything at this distance.

"All the dogs have been talking about it," said the mastiff. I heard him move behind me, and then he was standing over me. This made me nervous, but I quelled my fear and did my best to ignore him. After all, there was a good tail-length of clearance between my back and his belly. When his head poked through the branches above mine, we must have made quite a sight, if there had been anybody to see.

"Your friends?" I asked. "You are friends with the ghouls?"

The mastiff snarled, a bubbling, nasty sound. I dug my claws into the earth, to prevent myself from bolting. "No," he disavowed at once. "They're no friends to the humans, or to us. But they're easy to smell. I can always tell when some ghoul has been sniffing around our yard; all dogs can. We can't see them, but we can scent them."

"And they're gone?" I pressed.

"We thought they were gathering in force. The word traveled up and down Walnut St. that the ghouls were on the move. Every dog was on the alert. They take human children, you know."

"I know," I said, thinking of my baby, with his yellow hair always needing to be groomed, and his squawks of delight when I allowed him a go at my tail.

"Then some dogs at the edge of town got news to us. They said that the ghouls were leaving en masse. That was yesterday."

My belly went cold, and it wasn't because of the wind. All the ghouls, gone? There had been ghouls on Burying Hill since the first body was laid! And then, what of my dreamlands vision? Had the temple spirits failed me—or worse, betrayed me?

I shook my head to banish such pesky thoughts, and resumed studying the graveyard. At this angle, and with all the trees in the way, I could not even spot its usual ghostly denizens, let alone the ghouls.

"I'll take a look," I announced.

"I'll come with you," said the mastiff at once.

I looked up at him in surprise, though from where I stood I mostly saw the thick, furry folds on the underside of his neck, and the spiked black collar that hung loosely just above his shoulders. Ah, dogs. Loyal creatures indeed—apparently, even to cats.

"Don't," I advised. "You smell like blood. They'll all come quick." I could see the mastiff's ears droop in disappointment. "But you wait here," I went on. "If the ghouls attack, then I can run back, and you can bite them. Ok?" *Thwap, thwap* went the mighty tail against the thick branches of the pines.

"You're not going," said Dot.

My ears flattened, and my eyes slitted. "Says who?"

"Me," said Dot.

"Oh? And who made you a god?"

"Nobody," Dot admitted. "But *you* are as fat as two cats—"

"It's not fat, it's fur! Damn it, Dot, you know that!"

"And a dark tabby to boot," Dot continued unperturbed. "Let the snow-colored cat go first." Stealthily she slipped from our evergreen hideout, and slunk across the slushy street, which was brightly and unfortunately lit by the rose-gray winter sky.

"Snow-colored. Hmph," I said, watching her go. *"That's* a bit of an exaggeration."

"I notice you're not following," said Libby, with an air of mischief.

"I didn't say she was wrong," I told him. "I said she was hyperbolic."

"Hyper what? What is hyper?" asked the mastiff, obviously not following our rapid exchange.

"She's a dirty liar," I explained to the dog.

"She is?" he asked, evidently confused.

I'd momentarily lost sight of Dot, but then her head peeked around from behind a parked car. I accepted the implicit summons, and skittered rapidly across the street, belly low, aiming for the nearest car.

Dot, by contrast, ambled over casually. "It's empty," she said. "The dog was right. The ghouls have left."

I crouched at the top of the hill and surveyed the graveyard for myself. As I did, it began to snow again—huge, delicate flakes of wonder. Peering through the gathering snowstorm, I looked for That Which Cannot Be Seen. Ghostly figures drifted, walking through trees that had grown since their time, weeping and raging over misfortunes now quite lost to history. As they glided upon their parallel track to the realm of the living, I caught something Dot had missed:

I saw the albino ghoul loping up a distant hillside, heading toward the bare-branched wood.

It was my vision, just as I'd seen it in the divining pool at the temple. Everything was correct—the snow, the sky, the stone cross, and the single, distant ghoul in retreat. The spirits had not failed me after all. They had, indeed, granted me a moment of precious foresight.

So what the *hell* did it mean?

In truth, I was more puzzled than ever. The ghouls were allied with the night-gaunts in the distant dreamlands of their origin; they should have been responsible for bringing them here, into the material world. Yet I was watching a ghoul, evidently among the last, abandon its ancestral home...while the night-gaunts, and all the rest of the creatures bedeviling Kingsport, remained. Not to mention the slips in time, the queer glimpses of alternate realities, etcetera, etcetera.

What did it all mean? Why had the spirits shown me *this* scene, of all things?

"So what does this mean?" Libby chimed in plaintively from behind me. "If the ghouls are gone? The night-gaunts are still here. There are *seventeen* around my house, Dot. Seventeen!"

The distant ghoul entered the wood, disappearing from my gaze, just as I blinked in revelation. Oh, bless the spirits of the blasted temple, hidden among the marshes! Bless the dark viewing pool and its forbidden glimpses into the future! I would return with offerings piled as high as my head, and bow low before their generous wisdom for all my lives.

"I've got it," I said aloud. I sat up, careless of who or what might see me now. "Seventeen night-gaunts, Dot. Seventeen!"

"So I've heard," grumbled Dot. "What does it mean?"

That was the third iteration of the question, and at last I had an answer. "Listen. There was one night-gaunt upon my house the first time. Then there were three, upon the second occasion. What was the difference?"

"I don't know…" said Dot slowly. "You ran in and didn't come back out, and they flew off, so we watched for a while and then went away."

"Morwen was practicing again, Dot," I revealed triumphantly. "She was chanting in the attic. They were attracted to the magic!"

Dot's dark eyes widened in a rare show of shock. "So…at Libby's house…"

"*Seventeen* night-gaunts!"

"But Mark and Clarence don't…" Libby began, confused. But with quick feline comprehension, he soon grasped our meaning. "Oh. The *guests.*"

"Yes!" My tail quivered with excitement. "Who's staying there now, Libby?"

"There's been two men there for a while," said Libby. "Neil and Rob. They're photographers. But Spice, they've been there since November, *way* before this started."

"So?" Dot pressed swiftly. "A few weeks of scoping out the area and doing research before the campaign begins. That's how I would do it."

"And photographers would have an excuse to poke around out-of-the-way places," I mused. "To carry big bags full of equipment, and do odd things in dark alleys and shadowed groves." I searched my memory. "Can you remember what they were up to two nights ago?"

"I haven't the faintest idea," said Libby. He sounded miffed. "They were out late. Didn't get back to the house until almost dawn."

"Aha!" I exclaimed. My pupils dilated in excitement, and the snow glittered almost painfully bright. "I *knew* someone was up to some magic that night! I could feel it in my whiskers!"

"But *why?*" Libby wanted to know. "Why would they do something like this? They seem so ordinary. And at Christmas, too!"

Ah, Christmas! There was something to that, something I hadn't yet considered. Tilly and I had spoken of the ancient midwinter rites that kept our world safe, contained, and upon its own track—rites that had now, sadly, gone to rack and ruin. But there were other ways to bend the ancient power of Yuletide…

"And," Libby went on, in his new role as devil's advocate, "what if they aren't the ones causing all this? What if they're just practitioners trying to protect themselves?"

"Then they can give us a few tips," I stated firmly. "Stars know we could use them."

A long-drawn whine was carried to our ears by the whistling wind. The mastiff was growing impatient.

"The solstice will happen in just a few days," I said. "My guess is that, for better or worse, this will all come to a head then. Meanwhile, I suggest we follow these photographers and see what they're about."

"It won't be easy," Dot said skeptically. "Even with four of us. Assuming we're including Cinnamon."

"That depends," I said. "Did she join the King's court?"

"The what now?"

"Court, dear," Libby said with a purr.

"I *heard* what she said!" Dot's tail lashed indignantly. "I meant nobody told me a damn thing about any King's court."

"Apparently he's found a farm south from here where a goodly number of cats could hide," I told her. "We've been invited. Sort of."

"What good will leaving do?"

"He claims that everything's normal outside of town. Whatever is happening to Kingsport is *only* happening to Kingsport. So he says," I reiterated, unwilling to place much trust in the King's assertions.

Dot huffed, ears flattening. Her tail twisted and swept across the snow. "That jerk. He never said anything to me."

"Do we want to go?" asked Libby, his own ears swept back with anxiety. "Just for a day or two? If you're right about it peaking at the solstice, we could come back afterwards."

"What are you, a dog?" Dot demanded angrily. "We're not a pack. Do what you want."

I considered it. And as I did, another long, anxious whine from across the street stirred in me a sense of shame. I'd grown almost dog-like in this lifetime, I really had. My devotion to Morwen and her child—soon, children—was hardly properly feline.

Yet I remembered slipping into my baby's room late at night, for the very first time. I'd leapt into the tiny newborn's crib to examine him; seeing his hair was mussed, I'd proceeded to settle down beside him, and lick those few thin, yellow strands into place. He'd seized my belly fur with a shockingly strong grip, and buried his face against my stomach, just like any kitten nuzzling for milk. Since that moment, my whole heart had been carried in those little, sticky fingers.

Even if I abandoned Morwen and Her Husband to their fate, could I leave my baby to face what was coming alone?

I shook off the snow that had accumulated upon my shaggy fur. We needed to leave at once, or we'd face a difficult slog home through the drifts. I looked over my shoulder, at the hill where I'd glimpsed the albino ghoul, but the entire area was now obscured by falling flakes. The graveyard was silent, emptier now than it had been in hundreds of years.

"The ghouls all left," I said. "For the first time since the first grave was dug, there are no ghouls in Kingsport. Something very, very bad is going to happen—or at least *they* think it's going to happen. And I think," I went on, looking back and forth from Dot to Libby, "that if we leave, there might not be a Kingsport to come back to."

Long silence enveloped the three of us, as did the steadily drifting snow, which was now beginning to obscure the yellow glow of the streetlamps.

"I'd make Morwen leave if I could," I said at last. "But she won't. She loves that old house. And she's pregnant…"

"Ditto. Mark and Clarence will never leave their guest house. They've sunk too much time and money into it," said Libby. His paws fidgeted in the snow, as if they'd like to leave, whether he would or not. "I guess I'll stay and try to help them, however I can."

"If Lydia travels for Christmas, and she might, then I'm going with her," Dot warned. "But if she doesn't…"

"You'll stay," I finished for her, when she didn't.

"Fuck the King and his court," she grumbled. "I wish we had Big Red. He'd know what to do."

"Oh!" Libby exclaimed, bat-like ears sweeping upright once more. "That's right! I mean, we can't ask Big Red. But we could ask Tilly! Surely she'll know what to do."

"Tilly is dead," I told him flatly. "She died this afternoon."

"Really? Damn!"

"Getting back to the point, Spice," Dot insisted, "how exactly are three, maybe four, cats supposed to track a couple of humans? Libby, do they have a car?"

"Yes," he said gloomily.

"Humans in a *car* in this kind of weather?" Dot crouched down low, betraying her anxiety. "We'd be better off spending the time fortifying our homes."

"We can do both," I said. "I—"

Three short, staccato barks rang out from the evergreens. Dimly, through the driving snow, I could see the light turn on in the upper room of the house across from us. When another light turned on in a downstairs room, I knew it was past time to go.

"I have an idea," I finished. "It involves the dog."

"Of course it does," Libby sighed.

"But first," I advised, watching the porch light flood the yard, "we need to scoot."

9

Unspeakable

There were no night-gaunts haunting our roof tonight, thank heavens. Though Tilly's gift had replenished me for awhile, by now my very bones ached. I needed to curl up somewhere, warm, and soft, and quiet. Had the laundry basket been emptied yet? I would soon find out.

No sooner had I squeezed through the cat flap than a heady whiff of incense seized my attention. Dragon's blood again, same as last time. It was a little stale—it had probably been burned some time ago. But to what purpose?

Sharpening my gaze to See That Which Cannot Be Seen, I immediately glimpsed the faint—I don't know, what is the visual equivalent of a tickle? Let's call it a twinkle, though it resembles neither a star nor a firefly. Out of the corner of my eye I saw this 'twinkle' in the large picture window of the old parlor. I padded over and reared up, resting my paws on the glass to nose at this new piece of magic.

It was actually an old piece of magic, at least historically: a stone with a hole worn through it by the sea, and an old iron key tied to it with twine. It was the most basic of protective charms, the sort of thing anyone with a feel for folk traditions might dangle in their window. As for the magic involved, the 'twinkle' about it was discernible but faint, much like the lingering aroma of incense. It certainly didn't pack much of a punch.

Yet I was ecstatic, for this indicated two important developments: first, that Morwen had indeed resumed her witching ways; second, and far more importantly, she was at last properly frightened by recent events. Very well, let her be frightened. Every human in Kingsport was in over their head—it was just that most of them didn't know it.

I stole upstairs, avoiding the squeaky spots on the carpeted staircase. Listening at the door, I could easily discern Morwen and Her Husband's breathing in their own room. Satisfied that they were sound asleep, I padded over to my baby's room. Her Husband had closed the door, no doubt with the intention of keeping me out. Too bad for him—I had no trouble stretching up and hooking a paw over the lever, dragging it down far enough to unlatch the door.

There was my baby, curled in his crib, smelling of peanut butter and bananas and yogurt and whatever else they'd stuffed into him before bedtime, in hopes that he'd sleep through the night. He was lying on his stomach with his arms stretched behind him and his buttocks high in the air, snoozing as profoundly as an exhausted kitten.

The aforementioned aching bones prevented me from just jumping in. Instead, I took a more circuitous route, from rocking chair to bedside table, bedside table to changing table, changing table to crib rail, and from there into the warm, snuggly, baby-scented depths of his bed. As I settled my warm belly over his cold little toes, I again felt a twinge of shame.

We cats prided ourselves on our independent natures and eccentric ways. To be so wholeheartedly devoted to a human baby was simply un-feline.

The fact was that I'd simply gone too many lifetimes without giving birth. I'd been fixed in my last two lives, and had been run over as a kitten the life before that; my memories of my litters, and of motherhood in general, were growing too vague for comfort.

The day their eyes opened, that had always been my favorite: one by one the little blind faces blinking wide their gem-colored eyes, like flowers blossoming to the sunlight. That was the moment they became not just crawling, mewling, wriggling sacks of fur and instinct, but felines unto themselves. "The eyes are the windows to the soul," I believe humans say, and it's quite true—that was also usually the day they began to remember their past selves. In previous lifetimes I had birthed some truly amazing souls into this world, cats with ten or twelve or more lives behind them. All had thanked me for the warm, sweet welcome I'd offered them, with my womb, my milk, my tongue, and my love.

As I pondered all this, the door squeaked further open. I stiffened, ready to spring from the crib to escape Her Husband, then relaxed. It was only Morwen, wrapped in Her Husband's brown bathrobe.

You terrible animal! She scolded me in a hissing whisper. *I can't believe you ran away from the vet!* And then—*Poor thing, they told me a big dog attacked you! Are you all right, sweetie? Did he hurt you? Poor Pumpkin Spice...*

I purred reassuringly, and allowed Morwen to lift me from the crib. She cuddled me for a moment, rubbing her nose into my thick fur and murmuring sweet nothings. I purred ferociously in response, swiping my cheek against any part of her that presented itself: her shoulder, her ear, her hand.

And now, you naughty thing... Morwen plopped me on the floor, not even bothering to bend down and give me an easy landing. I fell upon my feet, naturally, but could not resist a sharp *mrow* at the sudden impact upon my weary muscles. *This ends today,* Morwen declared.

Uh-oh. This couldn't be good. Morwen began making her unsteady way down the staircase. I followed closely behind, trying to remain as near as possible, while not actually tripping her.

When she reached the kitchen, she picked up some things off the kitchen table. I craned my head back, trying to see what they were, but I couldn't until she headed for the back door. Then I saw what she carried—a hammer and nails!

No! I leapt for the cat door, but for an enormously pregnant woman, Morwen moved surprisingly fast. She also cheated: she grabbed my tail as I dashed away, hauling me backwards. I yowled and hissed, but it did no good. Blocking me with her backside, Morwen bent over, placed a nail against the end of the rubber flap, right where it overlapped with the door, and pounded it into place. *Bang! Bang! Bang!* went my freedom, as Morwen hammered nail after nail home. Not even my full weight was going to tear that flap free.

When she finally stood up again, I sat heavily and stared at my former exit, too aghast even to protest. Morwen, apparently done ruining my life, placed the tools on the kitchen table with a loud *clank.* Coming back, she bent down with an *ooph* and scratched me under my chin.

Sorry, girl, she murmured, stroking my back when I sullenly jerked my head away. *But it's dangerous out there. You're coming home all beat up, and there's other things as well...it's just not safe.*

Her meaning hardened. *So get used to it. You're a housecat now.*

When I didn't respond, she sighed, patted the top of my head, and shuffled back toward the stairs. I stayed on the kitchen floor, staring through the back door's cracked glass window, and watched a night-gaunt soar past the waning crescent moon.

* * *

"They're not going to let you out?" Cinnamon wanted to know. She was pressed against the screen in the kitchen window, her magnificent fur's pattern barely discernible through the thick netting. I was lucky the window was open, so that we could actually talk. Fortunately, the ancient oven heated the kitchen to an unbearable degree, even in winter, and Morwen was in full Christmas-cookie-exchange mode.

"No," I replied gloomily. "It's been a full day and she hasn't changed her mind."

"Did you cry really loudly?" Cinnamon pressed.

"Of course."

"And prostrate yourself in front of the door?"

"Yes."

"And refuse to eat?"

"Yes."

Cinnamon sat down carefully on the ledge and sighed in wonder. "Your human is really tough."

"She's scared," I explained. "Unlike most of the pinheads in this town, she knows something's wrong."

"My humans know something is wrong," Cinnamon contradicted me. "They're getting in a feng shui expert after the New Year."

"I think this is a little bigger than rearranging a house."

"And the grandmother has been burning extra incense at the altar every night, and chanting. And she talked on the phone with some Taoist priestess who's sending a Fu through the mail."

"Well, all right, so she knows something's up," I conceded grudgingly. "That's better than nothing. But look at Mark and Clarence. We think the photographers living in their house are the cause of it all, and they're—"

"Caroling," Cinnamon supplied helpfully.

"Seriously?"

"Tonight, and every night until Christmas."

"That's unhelpful." I paused to nibble at an itchy spot on my shoulder, and then lick the disordered fur back down. "Remind me what day this is, would you?"

"Two days until the new moon," Cinnamon replied promptly. "Coming next is the Frozen Mouse Moon."

"I knew *that*," I told her irritably. Like most cats, I knew the movements of the moon instinctively, right down to the tips of my whiskers. "I meant, how long until the solstice?"

"Also two days."

I blinked at her and sat up a little straighter. "The solstice and the new moon coincide? Are you sure?"

"Yes." Cinnamon tilted her delicate head back, apparently engaged in examining her memories. "I'm pretty sure, anyway."

"A new moon on the solstice. How often does that happen?"

Cinnamon pondered, cocking her head to one side. "I'm not

sure. We'd need a cat who knows more about the stars. Maybe in the dreamlands?" she suggested.

"Maybe. I don't know, it might be nothing. But," I added, with a self-pitying little *mrrow,* "I might as well go there and check. It's not as if I have anything better to do."

"Don't worry," Cinnamon consoled me. "Morwen's got to give in if you just keep making a fuss. You'll be out in no time."

I was less certain of that. Morwen had occasionally made noises about keeping me indoors, especially as the risks for free-roaming cats had become more widely publicized, but I'd never seen her so determined.

"Tell me at least," I said, changing the subject, "that the dog thing is working."

'The dog thing' was a plan hastily communicated to Dot the morning after my imprisonment, when she'd dropped by on her hunting rounds. I'd spoken to her through the tiny crack under the front door, and explained the idea I'd conceived at the graveyard: that though four cats could not hope to closely follow humans in cars, dogs might be able to scent them, and track them in that fashion. What was more, it was evident that the dog communication network was much tighter and swifter than that of the cats. Should they be willing to cooperate, they might be able to provide us with valuable information on the whereabouts and doings of the "photographers."

"Eh, sort of. Dot went to visit the mastiff twice, but so far he's just said that the humans drive around a lot. But he says the dogs are watching, and willing to help. If they find anything, they're supposed come here—she's told the mastiff where you live."

"A fat lot of good that will do." Abruptly my temper boiled over, and I smacked at the screen in rage. "Of all the times to get overprotective, Morwen!"

Oh, what are you hissing about now? Morwen asked, bustling into the kitchen. She was covered from head to toe in flour, and wiped her sweaty forehead with an equally sweaty forearm, resulting in a smearing of flour in her dark hair. *Aw, who's your friend?*

Cinnamon turned on the charm, purring, walking back and forth on the ledge, and pressing herself against the mesh. Morwen tickled her a little through the screen before trying to pet me. I dodged the caress, and not only because I didn't want flour in my fur.

Oh, don't be mad, she clucked at me. *I know you want to play with your friends, but it's really not safe out there. You go on home,* she addressed Cinnamon. *Go get inside. It's too cold for a short-haired cat, and besides...* She let the sentence trail off, with a frown, before turning back to one of several mixing bowls.

"When is she due?" Cinnamon asked.

"Early spring," I said. "Another three moons, at most, and probably before then. My baby—I mean, her son—was early."

"Good luck," said Cinnamon, and I knew she didn't just mean for the baby's birth.

"Thanks," I told her. She gathered herself, preparing to spring from the ledge, but I stopped her. "So, by the way…you didn't decide to join the King's court? And head south?"

She blinked tawny eyes at me. "What? No."

"He didn't ask you?"

"Of course he did. But I want to help."

With that simple assertion, she leapt gracefully down, and loped off through the deepening snow. My ears twitched in puzzlement as I watched her go. I never could guess what that cat would do next.

Wet, heavy snow had fallen quite steadily—if slowly—ever since last night, resulting in drifts so deep, and roads so icy, that Morwen had actually stayed home for once. Hence, the baking fit. I stared out at the drifting snowflakes, and then through them to the gray sky overhead, where I'd last seen the night-gaunt soar.

The new moon and the solstice—that is, Yule—would coincide this year. What did that mean?

***

Since I was a useless housecat now, doomed to file my claws on baseboards instead of mouse skulls, I left the overheated kitchen and did the only sensible thing.

I took a nap.

But not just any nap. I prepared myself for an epic undertaking in the dreamlands. I drank my fill of water. I crunched down as many disgusting shrimp kibble bits as I could. I used the litter box, and scattered its little crystals all over the bathroom floor, as a continued protest against my imprisonment. Then, having checked on my baby to ensure he was safe (he was yelling for cookies in his high chair), I stole up the stairs to the attic, to the door I was certain remained unlocked.

It was more than unlocked—it was slightly open. Morwen had indeed been making use of this room. When I poked my head inside, I could see, by the dust-filtered sunlight of the dirty window, that all the cardboard boxes had been pushed back into corners. The old chalk circle had been freshened, its directional and elemental signs scribbled anew. The mass-market grimoires hadn't been put away, but had been left stacked high upon her desk.

I purred as I strolled in—careful not to disturb the circle—and sprang atop her chair. The old desk fairly hummed with energy: if wood could purr, it would've joined me. Whatever consciousness a desk might possess, it, too, was pleased to be put back to use.

I curled up in the Morwen-scented chair, covered my nose with my tail, and descended into sleep.

* * *

Carter's sunset city wasn't actually a very good place to encounter new cats. We went there to refresh ourselves, not to strike up conversations. So I turned my dream towards Ulthar, and in particular to the warm, worn stone hearths of the Arched Back Inn.

It was crowded as usual, and for a moment I dithered at the door, trying to see both around the long legs of human customers, and the swaying tails of the cats. A particularly lush, golden coat caught my eye. There, in a prime place on the hearth, exactly the right distance from the flames, I spotted that old scoundrel Solar. He sat regally upright, chattering cheerfully at an awestruck white molly scarcely older than a kitten.

As I approached, winding my way past human legs, through chair legs, and over the occasional booted foot, Solar spotted me. The white cat followed his gaze and I saw (with no little envy) that she had eyes of two colors: one a brilliant green, the other an equally bright blue. Truly, she was a lovely creature.

So you can imagine my deep gratification when Solar dismissed her with a brief, "Do you mind budging over? This is an old friend I'd like to catch up with."

The white beauty evidently did mind, for she rose and, with her head and tail at an equally haughty angle, stalked off. I settled into her pre-warmed seat with no remorse, and greeted Solar with a quick sniff of his whiskers, followed by an affectionate mutual cheek swipe.

"I didn't know we were old friends," I remarked with a purr.

"We are now," said Solar, cuffing my shoulder playfully. "And we never finished our earlier conversation."

"No." I recalled the circumstances—that terrible fight between Morwen and Her Husband in the kitchen—and shuddered, wishing I could shake the memory off like water. "There's been trouble at home."

"Oh?" he asked, though I could tell he wasn't much interested. Probably the conversation he wished to resume was more self-indulgent talk upon his own exploits.

"You know a lot of cats," I put in quickly, before he could begin on any of his, admittedly fascinating, adventures. "I'm looking for some cat who knows about astronomy."

"Don't we all?" Solar asked, cocking his head.

"Beyond the basics. I want to know, what's the likelihood of a new moon and the winter solstice coinciding? I mean, how often does that happen?"

"Hmm." Solar closed his tawny eyes for a long moment, before snapping them back open. "Well, based on the larger cycle synchronizing the calendars of the sun and the moon, I'd estimate about once every nineteen years. Maybe more.

It depends, you see, on how you calculate the day, and how closely you require the solstice and the new moon to—"

"Yes," I interrupted, "but about every nineteen years, thank you. You're sure?"

"Not at all. There are *far* too many variables. Do you want the two to coincide between dawn and dusk? Then you might be doubling that estimate, or more."

"Oh."

"On the other hand, be a trifle more flexible about your definition of the 'new moon,' and it could occur quite regularly." He cocked his head the other way, ears crisply alert, brown-gold eyes taking me in. "Why?"

"I told you," I said. "There's been...trouble...at home."

I relayed the incidents of the past week as succinctly as I could. As I went on, I could sense the stilling of conversations all around me. Tails lolled and twisted with suppressed interest; ears casually flicked in my direction even as their owners studiously looked elsewhere. By the end of my narrative, the ten or so cats on the hearth and under nearby tables were a rapt audience—not that any would ever admit it!

Solar appeared to be pondering my story, his paws pressed tidily together in front of himself, his large, maned head hanging. I was patiently awaiting his response, and thus was startled when some cat touched me from behind. Not just touched me—put both paws upon my back!

I might have reacted poorly, had I not also caught the distinctive whiff of milk, and sensed the tininess of the paws that were buried deep in my shaggy fur. Twisting round, I beheld, as I'd fully expected, a very little kitten indeed, young enough to still be rather shaky on her paws. She was a tortoiseshell, with a distinct yellow stripe that ran askew of her nose, and had greenish, somewhat prominent eyes.

"You're from Kingsport?" she asked me.

"That's what I said," I told the kitten.

"I was in Kingsport, a few lifetimes ago," she said. The kitten's brow furrowed into fuzzy wrinkles of concentration. "Maybe more than a few."

"Did you have a good life?" I inquired politely.

The kitten slid down off my back. The wee thing, hardly bigger than my two paws put together, settled herself onto the warm stones between Solar and I.

"I did not," she said clearly. "It was a terrible life. But that's not what's important. What's important is that I was there when the trouble occurred."

"What trouble?" I pounced upon the statement as keenly as if it were a mouse.

"Around Yule." She yawned, exposing a very pink tongue. "The Dark Yule, they called it. The solstice without a moon."

"Tell me," the kitten went on. As she spoke, her language took on some of the rhythm and cadence, not of a spritely kitten, but of a weary old cat. "You said time has slipped out of joint? Have you seen streets and houses, or even animals and people, that have not existed in years?"

"Yes," I said, considering the spectral horse that had reared above my head. "Exactly."

The kitten sighed, tiny ribs visibly expanding and collapsing in an exasperated *huff*. "So it was when I was there."

"Yes, but…what happened?" I pressed. I glanced at Solar, but he was blinking at the fire.

"Nothing much," the kitten yawned again. *Bedtime,* I wanted to tell her. "The Dark Yule passed, and by sunrise all was as it had been."

"Huh." For the first time, it occurred to me that I might have been overreacting. Would this all really resolve on its own? "That was all?"

"Yes," said the kitten. "That is, except for the stranger."

"The stranger?"

The kitten blinked in affirmation. "*He* was found clinging to a spar in the harbor the next morning, half-frozen and out of his mind. *He* said he'd gone back to Old Kingsport, to the ancient Yule rites. *He* said he'd met his relations in an old house and descended to the crypt of the church, but the humans said his footprints only led off a cliff. In the end they had to take him away to the big hospital in Arkham, because he wouldn't stop screaming about the churchyard. I heard it all from the nurse's cat." The kitten stopped, her eyelids drooping.

So this had happened in Kingsport before. In fact, it seemed to be a downright regular occurrence, though Solar's astronomical babble had left me thoroughly confused as to *how* regular. And yet...

"Did you see any night-gaunts at that time?" I asked the kitten. "Or other things that didn't belong?"

"Not in the material realm," she answered. She paused to clumsily lick her paw. I resisted the very strong urge to put her under my own paw, and groom her properly.

"The ghouls didn't abandon the graveyards, did they?"

The kitten widened her already buggy eyes at me. "No."

"So..." I hesitated, not wanting to offend what was presumably an elder, yet needing to state the case. "It's not really the same. Your Dark Yule, I mean, and what's happening now."

"That's just the trouble," said the kitten gravely. "Why is yours so uncanny? The Dark Yule has occurred several times a century for three centuries at least. The ghouls never left *then."*

Ah! Good point! My tail thrashed across the stones, as I tried to puzzle out the answer. What made my experience of the Dark Yule different from this kitten's?

"Tell me, Elder," said Solar, speaking up at last, though his gaze remained fixed on the fire. "This man who says he went to Old Kingsport. He was a wizard? Or sorcerer? An occultist, of some type or other?"

The kitten blinked again. "I don't know. I never saw him myself." She licked her paw again, considering. "I suppose he must have been, to know how and when to slip through the gap, and physically enter the old time."

"Yes," said Solar. "I suppose he must have been."

There was a curious stiffness to Solar's way of speaking, and I stared at him with frank curiosity. The dashing cat merely dropped his head upon his chest, and resumed his contemplations.

"Well, that's immensely helpful," I told the kitten. "Thank you very much, Elder. I do hope," I added politely, "that this new life fares better."

The tiny tortoiseshell chuckled. "Don't you worry about me. I finally found my path from the Lair to the dreamlands, and I intend to stay in Ulthar a long, long time. I'm done with the material realm and its dangers. But I do wish you luck in Kingsport."

She twisted round to lick, very ineffectually, her fuzzy tail; once again I was possessed with the mad desire to groom her from head to toe. But I did not wish to disrespect her. "If you have more questions," the kitten added, "they call me 'Bug' in this lifetime. I'm never far from here."

"Thank you," I responded, with genuine warmth—it was

a profoundly generous offer. Most cats do not like to incur future impositions, or even the chance of them. I dipped my head low, and got to my feet.

"I'll walk you out," said Solar at once, also rising, so suddenly he nearly knocked the feeble little kitten over. I glanced back to see Bug, apparently unperturbed, settling back down upon the hearth. Her eyelids fluttered closed, and her thin chest quivered with the rhythmic rise and fall of a purr.

"Your problem is an occultist," Solar told me, as soon as we'd stepped through the propped door of the Arched Back Inn.

"How do you know?" I asked, sweeping my ears toward him, the better to catch every nuance.

"Because I was a wizard's cat, once. I'm familiar with their meddling ways." His tone was so intensely bitter, I could nearly taste it on my own tongue.

I stopped dead in the street. One of the town's infamous three-wheeled carts was forced to careen around me—but the driver knew better than to curse at a cat in Ulthar.

"Did your wizard...meddle?" I probed.

"Of course," said Solar, with a hint of a hiss. The fur on his back lifted, just a little. Stepping forward, I nudged him out of the street, into a nearby alley too small for carts.

The friendly bumping of shoulders seemed to take him a little out of himself, and his fur rested flat once more. His tail lingered over my back, entwining with my own. "Perhaps my views are unduly biased," he went on, a little more calmly, as together we watched the colorful traffic pass us by. "But I truly believe that's your answer. Kingsport's troubles are the result of some human magical tampering, no doubt about it."

For a sickening moment, I considered Morwen, chanting in her attic. Had I unwittingly encouraged her to unbalance the metaphysics of our town, and crack open the gap between realms? No, I reassured myself, the trouble had begun long before Morwen had resumed her practice. This mess was the cause of Morwen's magic, not the other way about.

"I'm sure you're right," I said. "I told you, the photographers—"

"Yes," Solar interrupted, "but I don't believe you understand how serious, how sinister, their motives may be."

His shoulders hunched, and he crouched low upon the sidewalk, ducking phantoms.

"I don't know anything about Kingsport," he warned me, his eyes darting alertly from me, to the traffic, and back again. "But I know something about the old rites of Yule. Those are dark ceremonies, Spice. The things some humans venerate—that they sacrifice to—are unspeakable."

Solar shuddered from head to toe. I pressed against him, trying to comfort him through the sheer weight and warmth of my body.

"They pay terrible prices to acquire terrible powers. I know you hope to protect your family," said Solar, coming at last to the pitch. "But I'm warning you that you're in far over your ears."

"Well, I've known that since the beginning," I quipped.

Solar sighed. "Of course you won't listen. What proper cat takes advice, even from another cat? But just take this into consideration, Spice. In my last material life, I was a black cat, and my human was a wizard. I lived with him, and ate his mice, and sat by his grimoire as he summoned, for many long years. Then the planets aligned in a certain way, and a great ritual had to be done in haste. He needed the fat of three black cats…"

I leaned away from Solar, guessing what I was about to learn, and not wanting to know.

"I'd partnered with the cook's cat. Our litter of two was in the kitchen. Spice," Solar said quietly, his fur rising at the very memory, "they hadn't even opened their eyes yet…but our kittens were both black. He killed my newborn daughter, and my son. And then he killed me."

My ears were laid stiffly flat against my skull. I could feel the hairs along my tail quivering as it puffed.

"I'm so sorry," I said at last.

Solar shook his head, swinging his handsome, golden ruff—a color nearly the opposite of black, I noted. "I scratched him up before he killed me, at least," he said more cheerfully. "And I believe my mate did some very nasty things to his pie. But please, Spice," he said, resuming his former solemnity. "If these men are what you think they are, then stay away from them by any means possible. And if you must engage—and I feel certain, knowing you, that you will—then by all that's holy and unholy, take great care."

"I will," I promised him. I rubbed against him, and purred my thanks, and blinked myself awake before he could share any more horrors.

I sprang down from Morwen's chair, and stretched long and heartily, from my tail down to the tip of each claw. Morwen and Her Husband were cooking dinner, and the shrieking of my baby sounded over the top of their mingled voices. Meat smells drifted up the stairs, delicious even when spoiled by cooking, and through the dusty window shone a sliver of the waning moon.

It was good to be awake, and to be alive. I would return to my human companions below, and do my best not to think of two newborn kittens, and what had been done to them and their father centuries before.

10

Foetid

For a full night and a day I heard nothing from anyone. In the material world this was for good reason: snow. It had now snowed more than I could ever remember, and the streets were doubly hushed by both the holidays and the sheer impassibility of the weather. The plows did their work, of course, but only truly determined drivers crept down the iced-over streets. The rest remained indoors.

From the wide front window I observed our neighbors' houses. Pine trees, both real and artificial, were carefully erected in living rooms and parlors. They were strung with colored lights and hung about with shiny baubles. A wreath adorned almost every front door, and more lights were being constantly tacked onto rooftops. I watched the man across the street fall off his roof, in fact; luckily he landed in one of the head-high drifts his snowblower had created. When the kitchen window was open I could hear Christmas music coming from three directions, so that old-fashioned carols vied with the latest, ear-piercing hits.

This was all too little, too late. Plastic lights would not keep the dark at bay; cheerful songs would not strike fear into wicked spirits' hearts. Shadows roamed freely now, sliding their way up snowed-in streets, crouching beneath porches, inserting long fingers into the cracks under windows. Ghosts seemed more active than usual, too, and more attentive as well: a sour-looking woman in a bonnet, dragging a dead child by his wrist, stared unblinkingly at our house until I scratched a Mark under every window, and pissed on the front door rug. Only then did she wander off, pulling the young boy's corpse behind her. Unlike the grieving mother I'd seen in the graveyard, whose shade was trapped by her sorrow, I sensed that this mother was doomed to wander for darker, bloodier reasons.

Her presence blended eerily in my mind with Solar's doomed children, until I thought I heard weak, frightened mewing at every door. Once I was certain I heard kittens in the attic, and raced up the stairs, through the open door. What I saw was not the storage-cum-magic room to which I was accustomed, but a cold, cheerless garret, with a little girl tucked into a narrow bed. Her face was covered with dozens of painful white blisters, and she looked as startled to see me as I was to see her.

Kitty? she asked, and stretched out a trembling hand—but I'd already dashed madly back down the stairs, my coat puffed to twice its usual size in sheer terror. When I at last dared to creep back up and peek around the door, the attic was as it had always been.

Soon after that, my baby cried out suddenly, and I sprinted to the family room, fully prepared to do battle. There I discovered he was only shrieking gleefully at a TV program; still, I chose to take no chances. Positioning myself on the arm of the couch, I refused to budge from my baby's side, even when Her Husband tried to shoo me away. Fortunately he seemed unusually tired, and after only a feeble protest at my presence, drifted off to droolly, snoring sleep upon that same sofa.

Long hours passed watching my baby watch television. Growing impatient with the lack of communication, I kept trying to drop into the dreamlands, but I was getting too much sleep and not enough exercise. It was a downright chore to make it past the grim forest where unconscious dreamers wandered, into the more splendid lands. But no matter how long I lingered in Carter's sunset city, or roamed around the cobblestone streets of Ulthar, or even investigated the fish-laden waters of the Isle of Orlab and the congested highways of the great capital Dylath-Leen, I could not find my friends. From other cats I heard twisted and exaggerated (or sometimes dismissive) accounts of what was happening in Kingsport, but no concrete developments, and certainly no word concerning our two suspicious strangers.

By sunset on the day of the Dark Yule, I had grown quite frantic. I now paced the floor by the front door restlessly, for I had been screamed out of the kitchen by Morwen, who still baked with a fervor that bordered on obsession. Observing Her Husband, who couldn't stay awake, and my baby, who was pitching almost continuous tantrums, I thought I knew why.

"Morwen," I said, poking my head around the corner of the kitchen. "Are you still mad?"

She didn't answer. She was bending over (with some difficulty) to peer at yet another tray of cookies in the oven. Already the counters were heaped with foil-wrapped treats. She could have fed a holiday-themed army.

"Morwen," I addressed her again, sidling cautiously onto the kitchen's well-worn linoleum. "I know you're upset."

Damn it! Ignoring me, my human cursed and slammed a fist into the glass oven door. She continued to yell something I couldn't understand—probably something technical about baking (which I don't understand anyway). In answer, my baby howled in despair, unchecked by Her Husband, who continued to snore on the couch.

Morwen shouted something at my baby, and stood up—too fast. She put a hand on the underside of her belly, and groaned.

"Easy, Morwen," I cautioned, daring to come a little closer. She rubbed her belly, and lines of exhaustion replaced those of irritation…but her expression also softened, just a little. "That's right," I encouraged her. "Think of the baby."

I wound myself around her ankle, and purred. She reached down suddenly and seized me, lifting me up into a wildly uncomfortable hug. I endured, and continued to purr, as she buried her face in my fur and squeezed.

"Baking won't help," I advised her, though struggling to breathe. "Sure, the baby's crying and your husband's no help, but what's really upsetting you is the Dark Yule. Making a few dozen more cookies won't fix that."

I rubbed my cheek against her shoulder. She squeezed me yet tighter, her breath catching with tears.

"You need to use *magic*, Morwen. Magic would keep the dark out. Hang spirit-traps. Light blessed candles. Sprinkle holy water along the windows and doors. Clap your hands and shout if that's all you can manage! You made such a good start with the charm. Why won't you finish the job, and really ward this house well?"

Morwen kissed me on the head and dropped me back onto the floor. I grumbled under my breath, but followed as she scooped up my still-wailing baby.

Sprawling on the floor, I watched her sway back and forth with the hiccuping, red-faced child, murmuring sweet nothings into his ear. "I've done all *I* can do," I told her mournfully, despite knowing she could not understand. "I've laid all the Marks I know, and I've paced the doors and windows. I even peed on the hearth, which I know you won't like, but it's not just Santa that comes down the chimney. I can only do so much, though. It's *your* house, not mine. That matters."

Looking over the blonde, tousled head of her child, Morwen frowned at me. Her gaze wasn't well-focused, but her face bore a kind of listening expression. I clambered to my feet, trying to lock eyes with hers.

"Morwen," I called, as clearly as I could. "Can you hear me, Morwen?"

Morwen tilted her head and dug a finger in her ear, as if she'd suddenly sensed water in there. My heart stirred with new hope.

We both startled at the sound of a sharp, canine whine at the front door. Morwen looked surprised, but my faint sensation of hope blossomed into full-blown relief. It was the mastiff!

I raced to the front door and called to him under the crack. "I'm here! What is it?"

"What?" The mastiff, unpracticed at communicating with cats, could not interpret a merely verbal message. He needed to see me, too.

"The window!" I squalled, and jetted to the parlor, where I waited with my paws pressed against the picture window. I heard Morwen come into the room behind me, my baby still sniffling on her shoulder. She gasped audibly as the huge mastiff reared up, placing his paws on the glass opposite my own.

"What news?" I asked him, in my absolute best attempt at his language.

"The strangers buried things today. In four areas, at the edge of town. North, South, East, and West. That's been confirmed by six different dogs. A pit bull claims they climbed to the top tower of the old church, and two little yappy things *say...* " I couldn't help but purr at the mastiff's clear prejudice, and nearly missed the rest of his communique. "...they went down into the basement of the old library across the street."

North, South, East, and West. Above and below. The six sacred directions. Chills shot down my spine all the way to my claws, but these were thrills of victory. I *had* been right! Whatever the strangers' true motives, they were, at the very least, occultists. "You dug it up?"

"No," said the mastiff. "Not a dog I talked to would go near, and they all told me to stay away, too. Said whatever the things they buried are, they smell bad. *Bad.*"

"Of course," I said grimly.

"This day has been bad, too—and won't the night be worse?" The mastiff whined and barked, clearly on the verge of panic. "Even my master got scared. He's so drunk, I'm afraid he'll never wake up! Can't you help him?"

"I can't get out of the house," I said. "My human, she won't let me go."

The mastiff fell back from the window. "Then I'm going home," he said, his tail pressed against his belly. "It's not good to be out here now."

"No! Wait!" I clawed furiously at the glass. *Pumpkin Spice!* I heard Morwen warn behind me, but I didn't care in the slightest. "Get other cats! Dig the things up! Bite the bad men! Do *something*!"

"I can't!" said the mastiff, and barked again. "I don't know what you know. I can't be out after dark!" He began to whimper continuously, hardly drawing breath. "That's how Mo died! We never even found his body!"

"Damn it to the Underworld!" I yowled, and sprang to the front door. I scraped and scratched at it with all my suppressed fury and fear, slicing deep into the old wood, heedless of Morwen's admonishing yelps.

"Let me out!" I screamed back at her, twisting round to glare at her. "Damn it, Morwen, for all our sakes!"

Morwen stopped her bitching, and looked round-eyed at me, even as my baby began to bawl pathetically once more. Patting the child absently on his back, she came closer to the door. I paused in my scratching.

I focused upon her brown eyes with the totality of my being, and summoned every scrap of power my soul had ever possessed, in all its accumulated lifetimes.

"*Morwen*," I said. "Things are bad! But I. Can. Fix them. But you—you have to let me *out*. Do you hear? *Out*. I can't save us all from *in here*!" I slashed again at the door in my rage, in the violent need to be *understood* for once.

Morwen still stared at me. I stared back, breathing heavily, my tail puffed up, every claw unsheathed.

Slowly, she shifted her child's weight to her hip. Having freed one hand, she reached hesitantly out, and grasped the doorknob. I watched, hardly daring to breathe, as she twisted it and opened the door.

A blast of icy wind struck at once, surging forcefully through the tiny gap and flinging the door wide with a *bang*. Morwen started back, and I nearly did as well. It struck me as an ill wind, both in the proverbial sense, and also because it was so bitterly, bone-freezingly cold.

"Thanks," I said to Morwen, in a more natural way. "Wish me luck." Then, my tail firmly erect and my head held high, I exited the house with a quite passable display of feline nonchalance.

"Come on," I told the mastiff, who regarded me with awe. Licking his drooping jowls, he followed in my footsteps, as I bounded over the soft, snowy drifts.

I was halfway down the block before my mind caught up with my ears, and I realized what Morwen had said as she shut the door:

Good luck, Pumpkin Spice.

* * *

I'd thought things were bad inside the house. They were infinitely worse outside. The road was bordered with high drifts, far taller than the tips of my ears, where the snowplows had done their work. Operating against all of my instincts, we were forced to walk nearly in the middle of the road, fully visible to the living, the dead, and everything in between.

It was difficult to say if anything watched us, though, for in the gathering dusk, all was confusion. The boundaries of time and space were more permeable than ever. Motion flickered almost constantly in my peripheral vision, and whenever I jerked my head round to stare, I could catch just a glimpse of something—the rotating wheel of a carriage; the flutter of a woman's long skirts; a candle being placed in a window that hung, suspended, in the air. It was never more than a glimpse, though, and faded as soon as I focused, leaving only the winter street scene to which I was accustomed. Then I would resume walking, only to be distracted by another flicker in the corner of my eye, and another, and another. I'd gone no more than ten body-lengths down the street before I was utterly exhausted, and suffering somewhat from whiplash.

My plan was to look for the strangers at Libby's house, only two blocks from my own. If we were fortunate, perhaps they'd returned home after their dark work, and could be blocked or trapped inside the boarding house itself; a highly unlikely plan, but the best that had occurred to me. That scheme ended when we arrived at what should have been a four-way intersection, and instead saw six or seven different roads. Three times I attempted to select the correct route, and three times discovered myself walking down a winding dirt lane, or a weed-choked cart track, rather than a modern paved street. I felt fortunate we were able to retrace our steps each time, but feared pressing our luck. What if we began wandering one of those antiquated paths, and then couldn't find our way back?

The little kitten at the Arched Back Inn, Bug, had suggested that phenomena such as these were common during the Dark Yule, and that the confusion usually resolved itself by morning. Yet this Dark Yule, *my* Dark Yule, was so different from that of her memory, I didn't trust sunlight to solve our problems. If we lingered too long in another time, we might never return to our own.

So I gave up trying to reach the bed and breakfast, and instead huddled behind the mastiff, allowing his bulk to block some of the gut-freezing gale. I was beginning to develop a grudge against the wind; it seemed to have something against *me* in particular.

"Where did they bury them? The bad things?" I asked the mastiff.

"North, South, East, and West," he repeated, clearly irritated with what he perceived as my failing memory. I glared at him and he added, with some reluctance, "The western one isn't far from here."

"Take me?" I asked. Perhaps, if I could not stop the occultists themselves, it was not too late to disrupt their overall scheme.

"I can try," the dog replied dubiously, having just observed my failure at navigation. He turned and headed up the street, while I did my best to walk in his massive pawprints. Between all the distracting twinkles and flutters of those fragments of the past, I caught a glimpse of that wicked mother ghost and her rag-doll corpse, peering at me around the corner of the house. A shudder shook me from nose to tail, and I scampered up closer to the mastiff, treading nearly on his huge heels.

It was sheer luck that Morwen's house was near the western edge of Kingsport. Two rights and a left later—all of them, luckily, uncomplicated by distortions of space-time—we arrived at a three-way crossroads, just beyond the last street of the last suburb. It was formed by a small road intersecting with a bike path, and there was a heap of snow mounded in its exact center. I didn't need the mastiff to tell me we'd reached our destination: first, because he was shivering and whimpering, his tail tucked firmly between his legs; and second, because I too smelled the foetid odor that had him nearly piddling himself.

The dogs were right: there was a word for this scent, and that word was *bad.* It wasn't that it smelled *bad;* after all, even the rankest corpses and feces hold some interest for dogs. So it didn't make my nose wrinkle—yet it terrified me. It reeked of *wrongness*, if that is possible to comprehend. It invoked a sweeping, cosmic kind of horror the likes of which I'd never experienced. The picture that sprang into my mind, unbidden, was of the stars burning out one by one in an eternally blackened sky. Mere Death, by contrast, would smell sweetly wholesome.

My legs quivered as I neared the scent, but I forced myself onward, trying to breathe as little and as shallowly as possible When I opened my eyes to See That Which Cannot Be Seen, I saw—much to my surprise—absolutely nothing. No ghosts lingered here, no vengeful spirits gathered nearby. Certainly there were no night-gaunts. The very quiet felt unnatural, and I wondered if even those I feared, also feared this.

Holding my breath, I sidled closer, and dabbed at the pristine snow with my paw. Nothing bit me, at least. Gingerly, I swiped the snow away, trying to see what lay buried beneath.

The smell grew stronger, and the mastiff began to bark.

"Quiet!" I demanded. My own ears were practically welded to my skull and my fur stood straight out in every direction, but I continued to paw at the snow. When the smell threatened to overwhelm me, I closed my eyes and thought of Dot, of Libby, of Morwen, of my baby. Already, at dusk, I could hardly traverse two blocks in this town without being led astray. What would happen at full night-fall?

There, under the snow, my paw touched something soft. I opened my eyes, and perceived a package wrapped in black cloth, still half-buried.

Gingerly, with the very tips of my claws, I pulled open the cloth. Inside, I was surprised to see a fairly mundane collection of items:

A small compass with broken glass.

An old gold pocket watch, also with broken glass.

A sigil, written in flowing ink upon torn brown paper.

A collection of dried herbs.

A silver coin.

The fresh, bloody corpse of a domestic yellow canary.

A fragment of some greasy, greenish stone, with gold flecks and striations throughout.

Curiously enough, I could tell at once it was the *stone* that oozed the evil scent. The other objects were comparatively normal. The great clue lay in the condition of the compass and pocket watch, and it was from them that I drew my conclusions.

Inserting my claws into the very edge of the black fabric, I pulled it askew, attempting to scatter the collected items across the snow. A few things tumbled out of the cloth, including the fragment of stone, whereupon I was so overwhelmed by its sinister odor that I staggered away, gagging.

With effort I stumbled back to the mastiff and, after three great heaves, coughed a dripping hairball onto the snow. Though this made me feel better, I doubted I could return to disrupt the buried spell any further. In fact, I was having difficulty even persuading myself to turn around and view the scene; for whatever reason, I did not wish to see where the stone might have fallen.

The mastiff paused in his incessant whining to sloppily lick the top of my head, a kindly gesture I did my best not to dodge.

"You ok?" he asked, apparently genuinely concerned.

"Yes."

"What is it?" he wanted to know—though I noted he, too,

looked anywhere and everywhere save for that disrupted mound.

"A broken…" How did dogs say 'watch'? Or 'compass'? "Broken human things," was the best I could do.

"What? Why?" the mastiff asked.

"The bad men," I attempted to explain. "They want time broken. And space broken. So they do it to the things."

"I don't understand. What does that do?"

"It's magic."

"I don't get it."

"Most don't," I snapped. My nausea had returned, and I rather thought more than a hairball might come up this time. I did *not* want to taste that shrimp kibble again.

"But why? Why are they doing this?" the mastiff wanted to know.

How like a dog to get at the heart of the matter, and ask the one question to which I still had no answer. "I don't know," I admitted, swallowing my feline pride. *But I'll find out!* I added, in my own mind, and to the universe at large.

My mouth was full of saliva; I swallowed hard and willed my stomach to remain calm. "Come on," I told the dog, rubbing against his leg as I passed. "Let's go to my house. We will think of what to do."

The mastiff followed me readily enough. I hadn't intended to take him into the house—I couldn't risk Morwen locking me in again—but there was plenty of shelter amongst the trees of our backyard. It would have been enough to soothe the dog down and form the beginnings of a plan.

But it was not to be.

One moment, I was bounding through deep, wet snow, aiming for the golden glow of the nearest streetlight; the next, I was facing a stand of bare-branched trees, skeletal and ominous, their limbs whipping in the icy wind. I tried to turn back, only to discover behind me a rundown, Colonial-style farmhouse. Its unlatched iron gate swung wildly until the rusty hinges shrieked, but no lights shone in the house's black windows. To our left were snowy fields; to our right, a silent, towering barn. I looked up, and saw the stars emerging, shining brightly forth in the absence of the overpowering moon.

Full dark had come, and we were lost in a Kingsport that wasn't ours.

The dog lost his head utterly. He bayed at the sky, and dashed off in some random direction. I watched his large, clumsy form lope across that empty field, to disappear behind a row of trees that also shouldn't have been there.

As for me, I sat gingerly down in the snow, curled my tail round my paws, and wondered whether I shouldn't just go to sleep.

11

Furtive

Sleeping was by far the most sensible course of action. Wherever I might be in the material world, I felt certain I could navigate my way to the dreamlands. There I might collaborate with other cats; beg the wisdom of magic-users more powerful than myself; visit the weed-choked temple and its black vision pool; or simply wait out all this unpleasantness at the Arched Back Inn.

This tactic wasn't without its dangers, of course; who knew what might happen to my body while my soul roamed the worlds of sleep? I flicked my tail and sneezed, a loud sound in the silent farmyard. To hell with it! We cats do not fear death. Oh, it's often painful, and tragic, and certainly damned inconvenient; but really, when your claws are out and your back is against the wall, what is the worst thing that can happen? You die, and that's that. We've all done it before, and we'll all do it again.

Some of us even accelerate the process. I dipped my head in memory of old Tilly, and the choice she'd made.

Head still bowed, I flicked my ears forward. There it was

again! In the dead hush of this alien Kingsport, the faint chatter of human voices could just barely be heard in the distance. With no better option in mind—aside from the aforementioned catnap—I rose to see what they might be about.

First, however, I lapsed into a long, luxurious stretch, in defiance of the unnatural hush of that dark farmhouse, and my own uncertain fate. Then, feline pride intact, I sauntered toward old Kingsport, my ears turning this way and that to catch every nuance of those distant murmurs.

I soon discovered I wasn't really *in* Kingsport at all, but well outside it. No suburban streets here, only, at long intervals, dingy colonial farmhouses, barns, and outbuildings, all of them not yet old but already battered by strong winds from the sea. Many of those houses had lit windows, which glowed reassuringly golden in the moonless night; yet I could detect no sounds within their wooden walls. I stayed well away from them all, and kept to the rutted track that meandered vaguely eastward. At least in this Kingsport, though the wind still blew fiercely, the snow was significantly less. I was leaping through only an ankle-deep accumulation, not negotiating drifts taller than my head.

More concerning was what I saw when I Saw That Which Cannot Be Seen: absolutely nothing. There was no difference between my dull, ordinary gaze and the special vision of cats. The dark spirits wandering the streets, the night-gaunts flapping their membranous wings, the flickering moments of the past—all had mysteriously vanished. For once, everything in Kingsport was as it seemed.

Why did that worry me?

As I followed the barely-discernible sounds of human speech, Kingsport rose up around me. The rutted track widened into an icy mud road. Houses began to appear more regularly, then to cluster closely together, then to be interspersed with what looked like shops. Most of the buildings were in the flat-faced, many-windowed style of the colonial era, and all of them had lit upper windows—yet still I heard no sound from within. If I hadn't stopped to gingerly paw at the corner of one blue-painted house, I might have wondered whether this wasn't just another illusion. But no, the cold mud under my claws, the bitter wind in my coat, the creak of the wooden houses, the smell of the sea on the breeze; all of these were quite real.

So where was everyone? Were the mastiff and I the only ones to be caught by the solstice, and sent back to this previous Yule? If not, then where were the others? And if so, then where were the rightful residents of this time? I hadn't seen so much as a bird or a mouse, let alone a dog or a cat or a human, since I'd arrived. Yet lights were on in the upper stories, though I never could spot a shadow against the illuminated curtains. What were they doing in the glow of their candles, to sit in such profound and immovable silence?

A vigil: that was what it all reminded me of. But for—or against—what?

There was one exception to the rule of silence, the faint voices I'd followed from the beginning. I'd been gaining on them all the while, and though we didn't walk the same street, I could tell that they were nearby. It was two men who were speaking, their tones hushed, yet still all out of character with the deathly quiet of the town.

Stepping out from an alley, I had to suddenly twist round, leap backwards, and crouch in the swaying shadow of a tavern sign. The speakers were directly in front of me. It was mere good fortune that they hadn't spotted my careless advance.

The two men passed my pitiful hiding place with nary a glance. One was tall, olive-skinned, and had curly dark hair that was tossed hither and thither by the salty gale. The other was shorter and rounder, and possessed of such a heavy hat and thick muffler that I could say no more about him. Nonetheless, one thing was blatantly obvious: these men hailed from the same time as myself. That was evident in their jeans, their rustling coats, and the large backpack the tall one carried slung over his shoulder. I peered around the corner, watching them saunter down the street, and marveled at the difference between the wanderers and their setting.

Were these the so-called "photographers"? Were they the men who had buried the black packet at the three-way crossroads? Or were they mere lost victims of the Dark Yule, the same as myself? Only by following them would I find out.

For the second time I crept forward—and for the second time, retreated into the shadows. What had I just sensed? I lifted my nose to the wind, quivering with suppressed excitement. Yes, there it was again—a hint of tom-cat musk. I hadn't been wrong!

I quietly backed even further down the alley, and crouched down low beside the tavern wall.

As I watched, a few furtive shadows slunk down the narrow street. They made no sound whatsoever, but they couldn't escape my keen eyes and nose. I crouched yet lower, hindquarters wiggling, as the nearest prepared to cross in front of the alley. Just as she stepped into view, I attacked.

"Mrrrrreeeeooooooooooowwwwwww!" Dot shrieked at the top of her lungs. The sound of her yowl bounced wildly against the walls, multiplying and echoing all the way down the many long alleys that crisscrossed the town. I rolled off her and and hunkered low, belly to the snow, waiting until the last whisper died away. Nothing stirred in the lit windows, and the quiet voices of the two men carried on only after a brief, watchful pause.

When it was clear that nobody was coming, Dot reached over and cuffed me on the nose, quite hard.

"Ow," I told her.

"You deserve it." She glared at me before turning to ostentatiously lick her back, thereby demonstrating how little she cared about me, or my opinion, or anything, really.

"I *am* sorry," I said contritely. "I was just so excited to see you all." For by now, Libby and Cinnamon had crept out of hiding and come to join us in the dark mouth of the alley. "I really thought I was alone here," I explained. "Well, except for the mastiff, but he lost his head when nightfall came, and ran off on his own."

"Idiot," said Dot scornfully, now giving her fluffy tail a good going-over. "Where does he think he's got to run to?"

I had no answer to that, so instead I purred and swiped my cheek against Libby's, and got my ear enthusiastically bathed in response. Meanwhile, Cinnamon had already walked several paces ahead, and was staring after the two men.

"We'd better hurry," she urged, her striped tail swinging, pendulum-like, in her excitement and interest. "They're getting ahead."

"Are they...?" I couldn't even finish the sentence.

"Yes," said Libby, with some importance. "That's *them*."

"Oh." They weren't quite what I'd expected. But then, what exactly had I expected? I discovered I had nothing to say, and proceeded to duck my head under my raised foreleg, and groom my cold stomach instead.

"Come *on,*" insisted Cinnamon. "Hurry!"

"They're not exactly *sprinting,*" Dot told her sourly.

Nevertheless, we resumed following our villainous occultists down the winding, dirty lanes. We stayed to the edges and ducked behind whatever was available—a wheelbarrow, a pile of crates, etc.—but after discovering no response to Dot's howl, I think we all felt a bit more relaxed. As for myself, I was practically cavorting down the street. It was only with an effort that I stopped myself from pouncing upon funny little drifts, or biting at the snow, or leaping atop whatever tall thing presented itself. Such a display would have been undignified, of course—it would have been tantamount to admitting that I'd been lonely and frightened on my own. I could confess that to myself, but letting other cats know was a different question entirely.

"So how did *you* get here?" Libby wanted to know, while he and Dot and I paused behind a large barrel—Cinnamon was still further ahead. Not ten body-lengths from us, the two occultists were shining a flashlight upon a piece of paper, evidently looking at directions, or a map, or something like that. It was an oddly average sight, I felt, watching the two men huddle together against the wind, and argue over which street to turn down. It didn't fit this haunted night at all.

"Spice?"

"Sorry." I dragged my eyes from the two men to Libby. "The mastiff came to tell me about the humans burying something. We went and dug it up. It was a spell packet of some kind, and it had a compass and watch in it, both smashed to bits. Also this green stone that smelled worse than anything I've ever experienced." I licked my lips in disgust at the very memory. "You?"

"Well, I was at home, of course, waiting to see what Neil and Rob would do." Libby flicked an ear in the direction of the two men, who looked nowhere near to reaching a consensus. "Cinnamon came to join me in the afternoon, and Dot arrived at sunset." Libby looked at me sideways. "We'd have asked you, of course, but you were—"

"Domesticated," Dot put in. She'd obviously not yet forgiven me.

"Rude," I chided her. "But yes, locked in. Go on."

"And these 'photographers,'" he spat the word as if it were a curse, "came home just before dark, all jumpy and excited as hell. They were about the *only* thing that was excited. Mark and Clarence fought *all* day. By the time Neil and Rob showed up, they were just sitting at opposite ends of the house, not speaking."

"It was the same at my place."

"Awful day." Libby's agitated tail swept the snow. "I spent the whole time chasing *unspeakable* things out of our yard, and of course a night-gaunt flapped by every time I dared settle down for a nap. Anyway, those two came back, and we were going to try and trap them in the house somehow…" I purred, as Libby echoed my own, original plan, "but they left again almost immediately with that big bag. So Cinnamon and Dot and I decided to follow them. That was just around nightfall, and soon it was full dark, and the shift came." Libby sighed and looked dolefully around himself, his massive ears rotating continuously, as if to detect any possible shred of sound. "And here we are."

"By the way," said Dot, "you notice something odd?"

"Dot," I said, "we're wandering around a Kingsport that existed almost four hundred years before our current lifetimes.

You're going to need to be more specific."

"I'll show you." Dot stepped forward into the street, where the occultists had just passed. Boldly, she sat down in the snow, her tail curled about her paws. "Look closely."

The sky was dark except for the stars, but the golden windows in the upper stories lit the snow well enough. I'm embarrassed to admit that it took me a long moment to perceive what Dot, the consummate hunter, had already spotted.

"No tracks," I said, with wonder. "Neither yours, nor theirs."

"Exactly," said Dot.

"What does it mean?" Libby wanted to know, looking from the virgin snow, to Dot, to me.

"I don't know. Dot, what does it mean?" I asked her.

"How should I know?" she snapped. "This is your circus, not mine."

"I did *say* I was sorry for pouncing on you."

"*Hmph.*" She sauntered past with both head and tail upright. I sighed and padded after her, leaving no footprints in the soft, yielding snow. I know. I checked.

* * *

The two occultists walked on for some time. The town's eerie, unbroken silence had some effect upon them—though they talked all the while, their voices gradually grew more and more hushed. By the time they turned down the final, narrow lane, they were just whispering to each other.

The street they chose was grassy and unused, and the

antiquated houses all had jutting second stories that nearly kissed each other overhead. The effect was of a wooden tunnel, and the wind made the houses groan. I eyed the many lit upper windows uneasily—it was hard to shake the impression of being closely observed by unseen eyes. The shorter, rounder occultist often glanced upwards as well, and I thought perhaps he felt similarly. Yet the two pressed on, leaving no prints behind them, until they reached the seventh house on the left. Then the tall one climbed the double flight of steps, with their elaborate iron railings, and knocked firmly upon the door. The *rat-tat-tat* of his fist made his companion jump, and, I'm ashamed to admit, it did the same to me.

We cats found shelter on the other side of the street, shielded from view by another double staircase leading to another high door. Peering around the railings, we observed the door open—first just a crack, and then wide. Golden light spilled out in a rectangle from the open door, illuminating the features of our occultists, but leaving the face of the house's occupant in shadow. All we could see was that he was a tall, elderly man who, despite his old-fashioned nightgown and shabby slippers, had an air of authority.

He stood silently, and asked no questions. The two men spoke to him, yet he still did not reply. Rather, he produced a wax frame and a stylus, such as I had not seen in many lifetimes, and made his scratches across the wax, which he then showed to our occultists. They nodded eagerly, more explanations were made, and then the gowned man stepped aside, and ushered them genteelly into his house.

A vivid memory arose without warning, from a long-ago lifetime I only dimly recalled. A mother was sitting by the fireside with her son; she wore a gown and a white cap, and he had on an absurd outfit that ran heavy to the velvet and ribbons. I myself, a trim little white kitten, lay by the hearth and purred at the warmth, and the boy's fingers in my fur, and my mistress's voice alike.

A book was open upon the woman's knee, and she read to the little boy, one delicate finger held up in mock-stern warning:

Will you walk into my parlour?" said the Spider to the Fly,
 'Tis the prettiest little parlour that ever you did spy,
 The way into my parlour is up a winding stair,
 And I've a many curious thing to show when you are there.

"But of course," Libby answered, and it was only then I realized I'd recited the half-remembered poem aloud.

"Yes," said ever-practical Dot. "But what do we do now?"

I didn't answer immediately; I was trying to capture a few last floating shreds of memory. I could see the boy turned a man; I felt his warm hand upon me, stroking my old bones, just before he'd left…he'd left…for what? For the sea? For war? I hissed in frustration as the recollection withered. All I could remember was the mother, age equally upon *her* bones, sitting upon that same chair and weeping in the bitter depths of the night.

"Spice?" Libby asked. "What's the plan?"

I shook my head and twitched my ears, trying to shake loose the ache of half-forgotten grief. "We go in," I said, without any consideration at all.

"What?" the other cats asked as one, astonished, but I was already slinking across the street. Perhaps it was foolhardy, but I was driven to it by the memory of my previous mistress's racking sobs. Stars forbid I have cause to grieve like that; better to die boldly, than live to regret one's losses.

I could hear Dot cursing behind me, but I was already beside the stairs. I reared onto my hind legs and braced myself against the wall, straining to peer into the window. My view was blocked by a thick green curtain, but just as the wind moaned round the corner, I rather thought I saw the curtain stir. Was the window actually open in this weather? Could we get inside?

I hesitated for only an instant before gathering myself and leaping upon the windowsill. I heard Libby hiss in shock across the street, but the deed was done. If something saw me, so be it.

The curtain rippled again in the wind—the window was, indeed, open! I peered inside and discovered that the curtain extended all the way to the floor. As quietly as possible, I eased myself down to the old wooden floorboards, doing my best to keep my bulk behind the curtain's billowing length. There, half-smothered by dusty fabric, I paused. When I was not greeted by cries of "Out, cat!" or "Shoo, shoo!" I dared to peep around the curtain's edge. From there, I took in the room.

First of all, it smelled nasty: an indefinable odor of decay permeated the place. I wrinkled my nose and sniffed heartily, trying to puzzle it out. *Rot*, the scent said to me. But it wasn't the odor of rotten wood, or even of rotten meat. There was something cold and earthy to it, yet it was far from the healthy scent of leaves decaying into soil. Besides, the room itself seemed hardly conducive to rot, being scarcely warmer than the winter weather outside. The enormous fireplace, though stacked with logs, was dark and cold, and the entire area was lit only by lonely, flickering candles.

My ears twitched at a familiar sound, though it took me a moment to place it—yes, that repetitive, whispery whirring was the noise of a spinning-wheel, something I hadn't heard in lifetimes. It was actually so dark, however, and the room so crowded with hard, comfortless wooden furniture, that it took me a long moment to spot the sound's source. It came from an old woman spinning in the far corner, who wore a bonnet and a shawl, and was fortunately both busy at her work and facing away from me. The two occultists also had their backs to me, in order to examine the tall bookshelves on either side of that lifeless hearth. With some satisfaction, I noticed they were shivering. The old woman, by contrast, appeared entirely unaffected by the cold. As for the old man, he was nowhere to be seen.

My great luck continued to hold, for amongst the other furniture in the room, a high-backed wooden bench—something like an old church pew, but taller—happened to face the curtained windows. It was a short leap from where I huddled on the floor to the bench's sturdy wooden surface. There I was not only quite concealed from the rest of the room, but could overhear everything perfectly. For some moments I crouched down low, listening to the whirr of the spinning wheel, and the excited whispers of the occultists.

I was just wondering whether I shouldn't try to signal the others to come and join me, when I caught slight sounds coming from the window: just the merest scratch of a claw on the wood, followed by the almost indiscernible brush of fur against fabric. Dot's funny little face peeped out from around the curtain, echoing my former movements. She turned her ears toward me, and at once I slumped over sideways on the bench, my furry stomach exposed and my plumed tail waving lazily, just as casually as on the sofa at home. That was to show it was all right, of course, not merely to demonstrate my immense bravery.

Dot's eyes narrowed at my display, but she didn't hesitate to slip out from under the curtain and leap upon the bench beside me. She was followed in short order by Cinnamon, and finally by Libby, whose ears lay prone in mute protest.

I was the furthest along the bench, pressed closely against its carved armrest. Since long minutes had passed without any human speech, I dared to peer carefully around the back of the bench. Our hiding place wasn't far from where the occultists, Neil and Rob (which was Neil? And which was Rob?) still examined the old books on the shelf. The tall man with windswept brunette curls seemed particularly enamored of the dusty volumes, and touched their spines with longing, lovesick sighs. He and his friend did speak occasionally, albeit in very low whispers, and though at first I understood none of it, as I observed them, I began to grasp the meaning.

The tall one said ... *by the mad Arab. Unbelievable!*

With a glance at the old woman—who never looked away from her spinning—he gingerly removed the book from its shelf and handed it to his companion. The other occultist had now pulled down his scarf, and I could see his face in profile: he had blue eyes, a large nose, and a square jaw, whose determined thrust was somewhat undermined by his scrubby, stubbly beard. He received the book from his dark-haired companion with an expression of mingled wonder and fear.

We've really done it this time! he whispered back to his taller friend, grasping the book tightly in both hands. I noticed, however, that he made no move to open it. The tall photographer took it back, with some impatience, and spread it out upon a nearby table, where he turned the thin, brittle pages with extraordinary care.

The man returned at this moment, from a dark passageway that, presumably, led to the house's interior. He held a candle in a brass dish, which he immediately blew out upon his return, and placed on the mantelpiece. The photographers both assumed guilty expressions; they might have been schoolboys caught filching candy bars. Yet the old man appeared to take no offense at their perusal of the ancient book. He merely wrote something upon his wax tablet, and showed it to them both.

Of course, said the tall occultist at once, clearly relieved they were not being taken to task. *Allow me to explain. We are devotees of the occult, and—*

And big fans, broke in the shorter one, *of...* And here followed a string of sounds I couldn't understand—a name, presumably.

We've studied all of his artistic works, the tall one continued, *as well as his letters and other materials.* He now produced a sheaf of old-looking papers, which the old man took. He gave them only a cursory examination before writing something else with his stylus.

Yes, indeed, the tall one affirmed eagerly. *He was a most accomplished member of your family.*

But his time at Arkham Asylum was what interested us most, his friend interjected once more. *We've studied the case records, and read his account of the Dark Yule. We tried to replicate...*

Tried to improve upon, in fact, said the tall one proudly.

Right, tried to improve upon, and, um, follow his footsteps, to come to ancient Kingsport, and... The round one paused to take a breath, and wrung his hands together in an oddly childlike fashion. *To most humbly partake in the great Yuletide rituals of old.*

It is true, the tall one picked up the thread, *that we are not your illustrious kin. However, we are devotees of the Great Old Ones, and—*

Here the old man made a violent gesture, cutting him off, and wrote something most emphatically upon the wax tablet. And it was at this point that I noticed something odd.

"The old man's wearing a mask," I whispered to Dot, who sat just behind me, and could not see. "It's quite a good mask, but that's not his real face, or I'll eat my litter box."

"I'd like to see that," replied Dot dryly.

"What's behind the mask?" Cinnamon wanted to know.

"How should I know? That's the point of a mask!" I would have growled with irritation had we not needed to remain quiet. Sometimes Cinnamon seemed so promising—usually just before she said or did something *particularly* dim.

Upon addressing her, however, I finally got a decent look at her mouth.

"Is that the key?" I demanded. "The talisman, I mean?"

"Yes," she said. The dark lump of foul-smelling iron was, indeed, clenched between her jaws. I could just see its uneven, crusty ends poking out between her black lips on either side. "And it tastes awful," she told me. "So you're welcome."

"Thank you," I said, somewhat hesitantly. "That was…very clever."

I'd just resigned myself to never deciphering Cinnamon's odd character, when the scene changed. The clock chimed, causing all four of us to startle. When the last vibrations faded, and I dared peer again at the room, the old man and woman were donning full-length, hooded black cloaks. I was afforded only a brief glance at the old woman's face, as she shakily lifted her cowl over her head, but that was enough to convince me that she, too, wore a cleverly-made, highly realistic mask.

It was evident that, while I'd been conversing with my fellow cats, the humans had achieved some sort of accord. The old man reached into a carved chest in the corner, and lifted out two more black cloaks, which he handed to his eager visitors from the future. They cast the cloaks over themselves hastily, yanking the folds in a clumsy fashion that demonstrated how unaccustomed they were to such garments.

As they struggled, the old man ushered the old woman toward the door. To exit, they had to pass close by the bench, closer than they'd come before. As soon as they did, I jerked my head back, nose scrunched, and licked my lips in distaste. It was *they* who were the source of the strange, foul smell of decay. I glanced at Dot, who stared at me wide-eyed, her own nose equally scrunched.

"They're not human," I said very quietly.

"Not anymore," she agreed, licking her paw and passing it repeatedly over her nose.

By the time our two modern occultists were properly arrayed, only the old man waited by the door. He was carrying a book under his arm—the same book, I believe, the tall occultist had been so eager to read. The old man picked a lit lantern off the table, and beckoned the two newcomers to follow him.

"Come on, then!" said Libby, as soon as the door closed. He was the first out the window, but the rest of us were close behind. My paws had just touched the snow (though they still left no mark—I checked) as the old man's swaying lantern rounded the corner.

"We'd better not lose sight of them," I said, moving purposefully down the street.

"Spice," said Dot behind me.

"What?" I asked.

"Look at the windows."

At first I was confused, and looked to the window behind us, the slightly open one we'd just exited. Then I caught sight of Dot, her head tilted far back, her eyes fixed upon the overhanging upper stories of the close-built houses. I followed her gaze, and realized that the previously lit windows were now all dark.

"Hmm," I said. I slipped to the corner, and poked my head around. I could see the little hooded and cloaked procession moving up the street, toward the center of town; they were well-lit by the lantern the masked man carried. But as they passed each house, one by one, the lights in the upper stories were extinguished. In that fashion, they carried darkness with them all the way up the road, until the only glow left was their single candle, burning in its glass cage. Yet once the windows were black, it was possible to see other bobbing, flickering lights in the distance, winding their way through Kingsport's many paths.

"Well. This is odd," I said.

"What about this isn't?" Libby complained, moving up beside me. His bat-like ears swiveled forward, then back. "And still no sound. Except for Neil and Rob, of course. Those two just can't shut up, can they?"

"Which one is Neil, and which one is Rob?" I wanted to know.

"Does it matter?" Libby said in a sniffy way, and quick-trotted past me. I was beginning to see he'd taken the presence of two occultists in *his* house rather personally. I suppose I would have felt the same.

To myself I resolved to call the tall one Rob, and the short one Neil. If I was wrong, who was to know?

"What do we do?" Cinnamon was asking, as I pursued that somewhat trivial line of thought.

"Follow them," said Dot at once. "They're the only ones who know how to get out of here."

"And we can finally figure out what they're doing!" Cinnamon was hopeful.

"Maybe they're having a tea party," I suggested.

Dot glared at me. "Why do you always feel frivolous at the *worst* moments, Spice?"

I frisked my tail and leapt after the photographers, racing down unmarked snow that glittered in the faint light of the stars. I could hear my heartbeat in my ears, and the snow smelled fresh after the stench of that room. My tail was fully puffed and quirked from side to side with a mind of its own.

"Fey," I admitted, forcing myself to slow to a mere trot. "Feeling fey, Spice. This is not a good sign." Yet all the wise words couldn't keep my blood from surging, making my ears ring.

Was this an oracular sensation, predicting my imminent demise? I'd reacted to the vague sense of oncoming death in this fashion before. Or was it just the relief of *finally* approaching the truth of the Dark Yule, after long days of worry and speculation?

"You've lost your mind," Libby declared, breathing heavily, as he and the others caught up with me.

"The lights are still going out," Dot observed. Indeed, the cloaked foursome were about a block ahead, and we could watch the windows blacken as they passed.

"Look," said Cinnamon, but we'd all already seen several doors open. More robed and cowled figures stepped silently from their darkened houses, to join the lantern-lit procession. People didn't emerge from every house—but they came from quite a few. Judging by the distant lights I could see twinkling their way up the hill, many others around town were doing the same.

"They're headed toward the old church," said Dot, who apparently could navigate even centuries-earlier version of Kingsport with complete ease. "At the top of Central Hill."

We followed, with a caution that began to seem unnecessary. We left no tracks, and neither did they. We made no sound, and neither did they. But their numbers grew and grew as they proceeded through the winding streets of Kingsport—always uphill, always toward the center. In the end, all the lights of the town were extinguished, and only the bobbing, swaying, flaring lanterns cast their wild light upon the faceless figures that lifted them. We could only assume the two modern occultists remained within the crowd, walking beside that old man in his curiously life-like mask.

The church was a black, spired shadow at the top of steep Central Hill. As the lanterns approached, they manufactured an artificial dawn: the white stone of the church was gradually lit from below, and slowly took on the golden tones of the approaching flames. It was a strange and beautiful sight, and even in our predicament, I was glad to watch it.

Slowly, the church's great red doors opened, and the cowled masses streamed in, taking their light with them, and leaving us with only the stars. Fortunately the doors were left standing wide, and none looked behind them as they passed between dark, worm-gnawed wooden pews. It was easy for us to slip inside the cold stone church, and to take a more circuitous route through the benches, always keeping the cloaks and lanterns in view. These formed a queue, and shuffled slowly toward the altar; the line grew shorter and shorter, but I couldn't see where they were going. At last, by putting my paws upon the back of a pew and peering over its top, I could perceive the enormous trap-doors that gaped just before the pulpit, and how the silent crowd descended through this subterranean entrance.

I huddled back down, and reported the proceedings to my fellow cats.

"Where does it lead?" Libby wanted to know.

"The crypt," said Cinnamon, sounding oddly sure. I saw Dot cast her a sideways glance.

The last lantern swayed and flickered down into the dark hole of the trap-doors. Like the red doors at the front of the church, the crowd did not bother to close these, but left them thrown wide open. Evidently, they felt no fear of discovery.

"Maybe we should wait here," Dot muttered, when they were gone. "They have to come back up sometime."

It was Cinnamon who demurred. "There are tunnels down there," she said. "Miles of them. They may not come back this way at all." She stalked forward, with her customary long-legged grace, to inspect the opening. "We'd better follow," she said, and commenced her descent without hesitation.

"How does *she* know?" Libby asked, but neither Dot nor I had answers—and at any rate, Cinnamon made a compelling case. Not to be outdone by the Savannah, I bounded over to the entrance, whereupon I promptly sneezed (quietly). That old reek of unknown decay was back, stronger than ever. Yet it didn't come from the trapdoors' old wooden stairwell, which, though it creaked beneath my testing paw, seemed quite sturdy enough.

"Come on," I told them, and followed after Cinnamon, ensuring that I kept to the side of the staircase, where there tended to be fewer squeaky sections.

The staircase was short, but we cats had fallen well behind the human procession. By the time we'd regrouped at the bottom of the stairs, only a few lights bobbed ahead. Judging by the lanterns' downward trajectory, and their sudden disappearance at floor level, the masses were once again descending through some sort of trapdoor. So where in the hell were they going now? How deep, exactly, did they intend to go?

Though the stone crypt was the warmest location we'd visited so far—including that comfortless, cheerless home—it was also full of that puzzling stench of rot. Even with my pupils blown wide to accommodate the lack of light, I could still only vaguely glimpse a few alcoves along each wall, and what might have been an altar at the far end of the low-ceilinged room. Meanwhile, the glow emitted by the departing lanterns dimmed with alarming rapidity, as the cloaked ones moved even further into the bowels of the Earth. Therefore, we didn't linger, but skulked rapidly in the direction of the last gleam of candlelight. In those faint rays we discovered a secret door in the crypt's floor, which opened upon a steep, airless spiral staircase.

Judging by the low-hanging tails and hunched shoulders of my friends, it was a path none of us wished to pursue. So why did my paw find the first stair, and then the second, and the third? Why did I find myself slinking downward in that dizzying spiral, hunting the fading glow cast by that sinister, silent parade? I meditated upon my own foolishness as I went—but I went.

Down, down we creeped, always so far behind we could

glimpse only a vague glow ahead, as weak as the first hint of sunrise—which hour was, in my considered opinion, altogether too distant. Where were we going? And for what purpose? My fey mood had quite died away. I recalled again how much I enjoyed living. And Morwen had just resumed her practice—and there was another baby on the way! It was a terrible time to die, I admitted to myself, no matter what brave face a feline might put on it. It would be tragically inconvenient to be slaughtered here, particularly if I didn't at least uncover the mystery first.

Dot apparently entertained similar thoughts. "Curiosity killed the cat," she muttered. I glanced behind me and saw that, while she padded bravely on, all of her shaggy white fur stood well on end. In her fear, she resembled a squashed-face little white puffball. Not wishing to discourage her, I decided not to mention it.

"But satisfaction brought him back," said Libby, supplying the second, lesser-known half of the saying. He leapt down a few stairs to walk beside me, and I rubbed against him in a friendly way, proud of his bravery. He was shaking from head to toe, of course, but each trembling paw still found its way on the stairs. I wondered if he, too, thought of his humans at a time like this. More likely (being a tom), he was imagining the many, many litters he had yet to father.

We soon discovered that Cinnamon had been correct about the extent of the tunnels. Side passages began to open up, long arched hallways leading from the endless staircase into who knew what black depths beyond. The first few were empty, or so I thought, until I (cursing my inattention) resolved to study the next one to See That Which Cannot Be Seen.

Another arched entrance appeared on our left, and I boldly

poked my head within—only to immediately confront a gleaming pair of yellow eyes! A nasty little face thrust itself toward me, barely visible in the stairwell's darkness, and chittered in a language I could not understand. I stood my ground, hissing viciously at the creature, until it slashed at my nose with its terrifying paw; then I fled, descending several turns of the staircase in a few lengthy, heart-stopping leaps. The increasing brightness forced me to halt, lest I collide with the cloaked ones, and there I waited, trembling, for the slightly-less-hasty descent of my friends.

"What happened?" Cinnamon wanted to know, her pupils grown enormous with curiosity.

"It was a thing!" I said, very coherently. "A thing! With a face!"

"What thing? What face?" Libby demanded, the hair on his spine rising with every word. "Should we run? Will it eat us?!"

"No. No." With an effort I sat, and forced myself to groom my shaking paw, somewhat quelling my own panic. "It wasn't very big. We're fine. Just…just don't go near those side-tunnels."

Before Libby could further pelt me with questions, I got to my feet and continued on, though I kept much closer to the center of the stairwell than before. I had no desire to describe the thing I'd seen, which though the size of a rat, and furred like one, possessed an uncannily human face—and a paw that was too clearly a five-fingered hand.

So preoccupied was I with the morbid memory of that unnatural thing, I nearly missed an important development: the staircase had, at long last, ended. Three steps more, and we would be standing on a stone floor—though that was all I could tell, peering around the sharp curve of the stairwell. What was more, the light had increased. At first I believed we'd veered too close to the procession; upon second inspection, it was evident that the source light was not the golden lanterns that we'd been following. The radiance ahead was distinctly green.

With care I edged further down the stairwell, though trying to stay well within its shadow. Now I could perceive that our journey had ended in a vast, natural stone cavern. The green light was coming from my far left, and the cloaked citizens of old Kingsport had gathered there; from this vantage point at the base of the stairwell, only a few at the back were within my view.

As for the rest of the cave, something queer covered its floor. For a baffled moment, I believed it was soft, white snow. Then I got a good whiff, and realized it was not snow, but a fluffy, hairy fungus of some sort, growing thickly on the eternally wet surface of the stone. There was more fungal matter on the walls and on the many stalactites, green in color and faintly luminescent; it hung in thick clumps like seaweed, or mistletoe. The flora all stank a great deal, yet neither fungus emitted the earthy stench that accompanied the cowled procession.

Cinnamon was beside me now, and Dot and Libby stood close behind. I spotted a conjoined row of red-banded stalagmites only six or seven body-lengths from the stairwell, which I thought might do to conceal us from the cloaked ones. Just as I'd nearly decided to attempt the dash—had, indeed, lifted the first paw—I became quite glad I hadn't.

The whole procession had been utterly silent throughout the night. Now, for the first time in ages, I heard sound: the thin whining of some nasal flute, rising and falling in trilling echoes that shivered through my guts. I jumped, we all jumped, and if I'd been in the open, that damned piping might have startled me into betraying our presence.

We waited, then, for quite a long time in the stairwell. The flute piped on and on, following no recognizable melody that I could hear; it never seemed to repeat itself, just continuously quavered out those spine-tingling notes. No other sound came, and at long last I ventured to steal out from the stairwell, slinking low across that noxious, fungal floor. A dozen swift steps secured me behind the stalagmites, and there I could crouch in near-perfect secrecy, with a full view of the proceedings. Seeing my success, the others swiftly joined me, and took up their own positions along the row.

Together, in aghast silence, we observed the ancient rites of the Dark Yule.

12

Gibbering

The first thing I beheld was a vast tower of green flame, flaring upward from a deep crevice in the rocky floor, and casting its sickly light throughout the cavern. Despite the fire's size, though, I didn't feel any warmth from that direction—it seemed the eerie, emerald flames produced no actual heat. Behind this bizarre fountain of fire, there was a river: wide, black, and oily. It wound slowly from the far right side of the cavern, and eventually disappeared in a dark, yawning tunnel in the left wall. It was in front of this river, facing the green fire, that the cloaked ones had finally ended their midnight pilgrimage.

We had evidently missed the earliest part of the rite, for just one or two cowled figures still tossed handfuls of squamous green fungus into that cold, blazing pillar. They bowed after making their peculiar offering, and joined their fellows, who stood in a semicircle around the spouting flames. Only one remained beside the fire, and faced his fellow worshippers. He lowered his cowl, and I beheld the old man, and his peculiarly lifelike mask.

What followed was the oddest church service I've ever encountered. It was conducted in utter silence, save for the continued droning and fluttering of that nasal-sounding flute. I tried to trace the sound to its source, but could only perceive a squat shadow perched some distance from the flame, barely visible even to my eyes. It didn't appear to be human, that much alone could be said.

It was easy to identify our two modern men, even in the midst of identical cloaks and hoods, because they were always one or two beats behind the movements of the service. Periodically the old man would hold up his ancient, moldy-looking tome, and the worshippers would bow. Sometimes they bent from the waist, and sometimes they went all the way down to touch their foreheads to the floor. With no sound or word to guide them, it was no wonder that the occultists were out of rhythm. Once, all the cloaked figures cast themselves utterly prone upon the nasty fungal carpet; by the time the two occultists got on their stomachs, the others had already begun to rise.

I was becoming, frankly, rather bored with these speechless proceedings, when the old man raised his hand. At once, the flute changed key—if anything, to something *more* obnoxious—and I heard the dim echo of far-distant flutterings. My ears swiveled frantically, trying to discern from where the noises came. Eventually I fixed upon the black, chasmal tunnel to our left, into which the equally black river flowed. Closer and closer the sounds approached, ascending the tunnel from who knew what Stygian pits. All at once I recognized the awful beat of membranous wings.

"Night-gaunts!" I hissed with horror—just as an entire flock burst from the tunnel.

Neil and Rob ducked as the ghastly creatures circled overhead, their wings flapping madly in the windless cavern, their clawed hind-legs dangling. Again the old man raised his hand in an unspoken signal, the flute ceased, and the night-gaunts began to descend. Each faceless monster crouched beside a cowled figure, and each cowled figure climbed upon the beast's back, straddling its bony spine between the two pairs of bat-like wings. With a mighty effort the night-gaunts launched themselves once again into the air, and streamed around the vast pillar of fire, to plunge back into the unseen depths of the tunnel.

All of them, that is, except for six. These night-gaunts had been waved away by their masters, and had resumed their flight unencumbered. Rather than rejoining their kin in the tunnel, they flapped hither and thither in the cavern, their great wings casting alarming shadows in the light of the emerald flame. As I watched their erratic airborne wanderings, I noted that the inhuman flute player appeared to have vanished. To where, and how, I couldn't possibly say.

Six night-gaunts remained—but there were eight cowled figures, for Neil and Rob were among them. The old man, his life-like mask smiling as blandly as ever, gestured for the two to lower their hoods. This seemed to alarm Neil, who kept trying to look discreetly behind himself, where several other silent, cloaked persons waited. As for Rob, the green light illuminated clearly his desperate expression, as he sent longing glances down the tunnel, where all the others had flown on their nightmarish steeds.

Let us go, too, Rob pleaded with the old man, gesturing toward the tunnel. There followed a long and, I gathered, rather flowery speech, for I sensed little meaning in it save the endless repetition of Rob's desire.

The old man showed no signs of being swayed—or even of listening. He was engaged in pulling strange objects from beneath his voluminous cloak, and setting them upon a nearby flat-topped boulder. It appeared the boulder had served as an altar before, for its smooth, polished surface was clearly artificial, and I spotted driblets of colored wax dried upon its sides. A second cloaked person, using a walking stick, scraped a large circle into the sand and fungus of the cavern's floor. A third poured liquid from a flask into a vast silver goblet, which was twice the size of any normal chalice, and heavily engraved with symbols I could not quite decipher.

The old man, having laid out his tools, gestured Neil and Rob toward the middle of the drawn circle. Rob strode forward without hesitation, and assumed his place proudly. His more cowardly—or perhaps wiser—friend entered the circle slowly. He took a somewhat circuitous route to do so, too, and moved rather nearer the altar than was necessary. I suspected him of trying to sneak a peek at the objects placed thereon, and I believe the old man thought the same. In response, the old man took a single, small step toward the altar; this was enough to send Neil scurrying into the circle, where he stood meekly beside Rob, his hands tightly clasped.

Once the two stood in the center, facing the old man and his altar, the remaining five hooded figures moved to different points along the circle. They were clearly taking deliberate positions, yet the spacing seemed highly uneven to me—or perhaps it followed an unfamiliar geometry.

With gestures, the old man signaled that the two occultists should drink from the goblet. Rob did so with an air of drama, cupping the large bowl between his palms and gulping deeply—I could see his Adam's apple bob as he swallowed. He sighed audibly as he passed the goblet to Neil, and ostentatiously dabbed the reddish liquid from his lips, a gesture that could not conceal his self-satisfied smirk. Neil, by contrast, took a much hastier drink. When he lowered the goblet, it seemed evident that more had gone on his scrubby beard than down his throat.

If the old man took issue with Neil's half-hearted effort, however, he showed no sign. He merely retrieved the massive silver cup, cradling the bowl carefully within his black gloves, to deposit it lovingly upon the stone altar. Next, he selected a thin wooden wand, carved from elder if I was any judge. He gestured for the occultists to kneel; when they had, he proceeded to make many signs in the air above them. Though it was difficult to discern the wand's airy tracings, I shuddered to recognize some foul Marks indeed, ones I'd only seen carved upon the walls of mouldering temples, in the more desolate lands of dream.

Now he silently bade them to remove their cloaks, and then their shirts—indicating all this with coaxing hand gestures, for of course that bland mask never moved. Rob flung his plain white T-shirt outside the circle with a flourish. Barechested, he again knelt before the old man, clasped his hands with reverence, and closed his eyes. He appeared to anticipate some kind of baptism.

"Hah. Lambs to the slaughter," Dot muttered beside me. Her back was arched so high, she stood nearly on her claws; it was only when I observed her that I realized I was doing the same. It took no small effort to ease my back down, and then to force my hindquarters to rest upon that soft, odorous fungus. Only when I was sufficiently relaxed did I again allow myself to peer between the stalagmites.

By then, Neil was fumbling at his own shirt, peeling it slowly up from his soft, hairy stomach. I doubted his hesitation to strip was due either to cold or to modesty (a peculiar human concept, anyway). Judging by his many darting glances in all directions, and the great reluctance with which he went down, at last, upon his knees, he obviously wasn't prepared for anything as innocuous as a blessing. I rather thought his expectations came nearer to the truth than Rob's.

Despite everything, I felt sorry for them—sorry for the tall, handsome young man with his hands pressed together in ecstatic prayer, and even sorrier for his wiser friend. As the old man raised his hands to the ceiling in silent invocation, I felt certain their doom was upon them.

After all our investigations, after all the risks we'd run, had we uncovered a pair of black-hearted villains, intent upon destroying the innocent? No. We'd stumbled on a couple of idiots, who'd taken their youthful dabbling in black magic a little too earnestly. Surely now they would pay the price, for venturing into the Mysteries too far, too fast—and then, that would be the end. Unless...

Unless this *wasn't* a sacrifice, as I'd presumed it to be. Just what was the purpose of this ritual, anyway? Were they truly about to be initiated into this faceless, voiceless group of worshippers? That I rather doubted. But many possibilities lay between warm-hearted welcome and brutal murder.

The old man lowered his hands. It was difficult to tell, given the fixed features of the well-carved mask, but I thought he studied the half-naked youths who knelt before him. For a moment, I envisioned myself in his place: I, too, stared at them with calculating eyes. Young idiots, indeed, but from another time, and another Kingsport. And to that other, future

Kingsport they would return, when the Dark Yule was finished, and the sun rose to illuminate its slightly lengthier day.

The kitten, Bug, had said that the Dark Yule's effects generally ended at dawn. But the consequences of this ritual—those might not end with first light. Whatever was done to Neil and Rob, whatever this peculiar ceremony entailed, the two of them might not leave it here, in this haunted time and space. They might carry it back to their own time. *My* own time.

Then the Dark Yule would not be restricted to a new moon on the winter solstice, and to a strange pilgrimage enacted in this alien Kingsport. Something of it would return with these two occultists, and take up residence among us. In what precise fashion, I could not say—but when this ritual finally finished, then surely we'd know the form of *our* doom.

If the ritual finished. My eye followed a crooked line of stalagmites that ran from our shelter toward the river.

"We need to stop this," I told them. "Before it's too late."

"What?" Libby demanded. "Why?"

I didn't wait, nor did I explain. I feared there wasn't time. Instead, I bounded forward, moving along the route I'd already mentally traced, trotting swiftly when the rocks shielded me from view, and slinking slowly across that disgusting, hairy fungal floor when they did not.

The old man raised his hands to the heavens twice more, making a total of three speechless appeals. Then he turned, reaching for the ancient, evil-smelling book he'd rested on the altar—

And saw me sitting upon it.

We stared at each other. He was as frozen in motion as the features of his mask, which I could see now was carved from wax. I, for my part, did my best impression of a Bastet statue, and fixed him with an imperious eye.

Then—slowly, deliberately—I stretched out a paw, and knocked the silver goblet off the altar.

A red liquid, too thick to be wine, splashed onto the dark, oily sand of the river's shore. The old man looked from me, to it, and then back to me again.

Kitty? Neil murmured. He sounded incredulous. I didn't blame him. I couldn't believe I was there, either.

The old man plunged his hand into his robes. Moving more swiftly than I would have thought possible, he withdrew a knife from his cloak, and lunged toward me, the glinting blade upraised. In the same moment, though, I sprang toward him, aiming directly for that terribly life-like mask.

Have you ever taken a Maine Coon to the face? It was a wonder the old man didn't collapse; he merely staggered backward a few steps, while my claws sank deep into the mask's stiffened wax. There was nothing to hold onto, and I was sliding down, so I twisted to the side, taking the mask with me.

I felt him seize my tail, halting my descent. As my full body weight descended upon my tail, I howled at the pain, and clawed madly at every scrap of black cloak I would reach. A miracle—I was free, and falling once more. I even managed to land on my feet, amidst a spray of oversized, white, squirming maggots.

Yes, that's right: maggots. I blinked at the writhing creatures, which wriggled out from beneath the ruins of the mask. Tickling along my back, on my head, in my ear—they were all over me! Giving way to instinct, I yowled and bolted, shaking myself as I ran to be rid of the horrible things. I didn't stop until I'd almost reached the stalagmites, when I couldn't resist pausing to twist round and bite a particularly wiggly specimen out of my back fur.

Wait a moment. Where was my tail?

Over my shoulder, I saw the old man clutching his bloodied knife in one hand. In the other hand he held my tail—my beautiful, fluffy, plumed tail—aloft in triumph.

The next thing I noticed was that he had no face, only a squirming mass of maggots where a face should be.

Throwing my poor tail violently to the ground, the vile creature whipped back to the occultists in the center. Neil shrieked his heart out at the sight, as well he might, and crawled away blubbering on his hands and knees. The other cowled figures stepped forward menacingly, halting his flight, and he cowered at the very edge of the circle.

The tall, wormy-faced being swayed in the direction of Rob, who stared open-mouthed, but had not yet made a move to flee. It stretched a gloved hand toward the dark youth, showing more white maggots crawling where the black glove didn't quite meet the cloak's black sleeve. The figure reached, and reached...then collapsed outward in a shower of the vile worms, which coated Rob's dark curly hair, his chiseled face, and his bare, hairy chest.

Rob's eyes rolled back into his head, showing only the white. He collapsed upon his face with a shrill scream, which was immediately echoed by his friend. Then, over the human wailing, I heard a gladdening sound indeed: the sharp, warbling yowl of a truly furious cat.

"Give her tail *back*!" Libby shrieked, springing from behind a stalagmite. Upon his heels were Dot and Cinnamon. As one they launched themselves upon the nearest cloaked figure, who reeled under their combined weight. Tripping upon the hem of his own cloak, the cultist went down. The hood fell back, exposing another maggoty mass. Libby shrieked again and jumped sideways, his back arched, his tall as stiff as a poker. It was good he did, for the cowled one beside him had aimed a blow with a dagger, and missed him by only a hair.

The measly stump of my tail throbbed maddeningly, and my poor head spun, but I wasn't dying yet—a cat always knows. So I turned round and raced back into battle, sinking my claws into the flying hem of the nearest cloak. Yanking it sideways, I toppled another mass of maggots, which exploded forth from the concealing hood. This particular fellow remained coherent enough to reached a gloved hand toward me, but Dot was upon it at once, sinking her teeth deep into the leather and shaking the whole thing like a rat. With no bone or skin to hold it together, the entire arm—if it could be called that—dissolved into individual, squirming worms.

Help! I heard Neil cry. I wheeled about, fangs bared, to see the poor fellow with a knife at his throat. This wouldn't have surprised me, save that the knife's wielder was Rob. Or was it? The dark, curly hair and fine frame were the same, and yet—

Come, my love, he called. *Come enjoy true flesh again. We can ride these boys all the way into the future. Quickly!*

Icy clarity descended, freezing me where I stood. These beings were not maggots, but merely possessed them. The spirit that inhabited the worms was capable of being transferred, and had already been so, in the case of the old man and his foolish, would-be devotee.

A hunched figure shuffled forward, and lowered her hood to reveal the old woman. Her face, too, was a mask, and I wouldn't have taken any bets as to what lay behind it. Neil sobbed hysterically with fear at the sight of her plain, slightly-smiling wax face, and twisted ineffectually in his stronger friend's grip.

A reek of urine hung in the air; a dark stain spread across the crotch of his trousers. His sobs turned to a scream when she removed her mask; really, I could hardly blame him.

But I wasn't really looking at them, I was looking *past* them, to the black river that oozed just beyond the bounds of the circle. There I could barely discern the floating end of a cloak, which rippled for just an instant upon the surface of the river, before being sucked down into the depths.

Just how many of the cowled ones were left? The old woman, advancing upon the piddling, weeping Neil: that was all. Libby and the others had eliminated one maggoty creature, while Dot and myself had destroyed another. So what had become of the other two?

There! That flash of yellow, in the murky ripples: was that the gleam of a lamp-like eye?

I looked from the oily waters to the tragedy unfolding before me. Rob's handsome, slightly arrogant face remained the same, yet was also, somehow, indescribably different. A new cunning glittered in those large, dark eyes, while his white teeth were bared in a smile that lacked all warmth. The knife pressed ever deeper into the soft folds of Neil's neck; with each pathetic whimper, Rob's smile grew larger, until his lips stretched farther than any human's should, a sight that made me bare my own fangs.

Was there anything left of Rob in there, or was it all the wicked old wizard? It was impossible to say—and I wouldn't wait to find out. I knew we cats might be able to knock a few towers of worms about, but a wizard possessing a fine young body—*that* we couldn't hope to best. At least, not by ourselves. And if we didn't kill this creature, this monstrosity, this death-defying *thing* before dawn, then by sunrise we'd be battling it in our own time, with so much more to lose...

Decision made, I launched into action. With a war-cry of my own (not a patch on Libby's, I'm afraid), I flung myself at the tall occultist, and proceeded to single-mindedly shred his legs from groin to ankle. I admit I thoroughly enjoyed the feel of his yielding flesh beneath my claws, the smell of his tainted blood, the exciting *riiiip* of tearing cloth. He yelled and kicked and stomped, missing my nimble paws with his boots by only a hair, but his hands were busy restraining Neil, and he couldn't halt the attack.

At last I sank my claws in that particularly tender place, and his cry of rage echoed from all the cavern's stone surfaces. Violently he shoved Neil toward the shuffling old woman, and rounded upon me, the long knife upraised. I dashed at once to the river—that disgusting, foul-smelling river—and made the ultimate cat sacrifice:

I jumped in the water.

The water didn't so much *splash* as *plop*. My head went briefly under, and the remnants of my tail burned as nasty water washed over the open wound. I resurfaced already sucking for air and struggling to keep afloat, my heavy coat for once doing me no favors. I did manage to turn my head, though, and watched the occultist wade in after me, fixed fury making a new mask of his face. I couldn't possibly paddle quickly enough to escape his broad strides.

If I was wrong, I was dead. If I was right, I might still be dead—but he would be, too.

A long, agonizing moment of panting, and paddling, and waiting ensued. Closer and closer he waded. I tried to swim away, but my paws just flailed through the water with nightmarish inefficiency. He was standing over me, that queer smile on his face, the knife still upraised. He was stretching out to seize me in his powerful, possessed hand.

A slimy thing brushed my paw. Just a touch.

Then, something that was neither man nor fish launched straight up out of the shallows, sending the black water flying. The green-skinned creature seized Rob's neck with webbed, clawed hands, lifted him briefly up, and proceeded to slam him downwards, thrusting him beneath the waves with a mighty *splash*. The occultist's feet kicked and lashed through the waters, while his fingers, hooked into claws, scratched madly at the green one's finned arms. In a moment, there was so much violent thrashing taking place I could no longer observe the scene. I could only glimpse the Deep One's dead-fish eyes, which gleamed yellow even in the sickly light of the emerald flame.

Gagging on the foul water, still paddling madly, I lifted my head and struggled toward the shore. I saw Neil wrestling violently with the old woman. Libby had climbed halfway up her cloak, and Cinnamon launched herself at the old woman's rippling skirts, but it was too late. Her body dissolved, spraying maggots outward, which coated the occultist's half-naked form from head to toe—just like they had his friend.

No! Noooooo! the poor man shrieked. He twisted round, and sprinted madly. At first I thought he merely careened blindly, but then I observed him deliberately change course, white worms still flying off his clothing, skin, and hair. He made straight for the mighty pillar of fire, without wavering, without hesitation. At the edge of the crevice, he did not pause, but leapt through the noxious flames.

The green fire put out no heat, that I'd noted from the beginning; yet upon contact, the pillar immediately set him alight, faster than any mortal fire. He passed through the pillar and landed on the other side, reeling, his hair blazing chartreuse, his pants smoldering olive smoke. On he stumbled, and fell into the river. A great cloud of steam arose, concealing him from view. I coughed as the hot steam roiled toward me, and swallowed yet another mouthful of disgusting water.

When the steam cleared a little, though, I was astounded to glimpse, not a burnt, blackened corpse, but Neil's intact body floating easily upon the river's buoyant surface. Eyes closed, mouth gaping, the poor soul slid headfirst down the dark tunnel, slowly disappearing from view.

Was he dead? Or merely unconscious? With a great effort I paddled closer, trying to determine which could be the case. As I neared the dark tunnel, however, a colder, swifter current suddenly seized me, speeding me toward the yawning entrance.

At once I fought it, turning toward shore and swimming with all my might. My heavy coat was dragging me down, though, and all the splashing and steam had left me half-choked. Relentlessly the current towed me toward the tunnel, pulling me faster and faster, until I perceived, with terror, the dark roof pass over my head.

Now the entrance was a half-circle of greenish light, growing smaller and smaller in the distance. All around me, I could discern nothing but darkness, endless darkness without relief. There was no shore to clamber onto, no boulder or branch to halt my passage. My paws passed through unsupportive water, again and again, while my head sank lower and lower. The river roared in my ears, and the tunnel's entrance was no more than a dim green dot far, far away.

I could swim no longer. I was going down.

I got a last gasp of air before my nose sank beneath the surface. I closed my eyes, and pointlessly willed myself to sleep. It was useless—the dreamlands had never been further from me.

Instead I focused inward, and watched my soul begin its long unraveling.

* * *

Light! Air! I gasped and blinked and choked, as a firm hand pounded my back. I was alive, after all. The mouth of the tunnel was still before me, taunting me with its nearness, with the possibility of escape. It took me a long moment to realize that the half-moon of light was *increasing* in size, not decreasing; I was coming closer to salvation, not floating further from it.

At the same time, I became conscious that I was no longer in the water, but being cradled in a somewhat squashy arm, against a rather spongy chest, all of which fairly reeked of delicious fish. It was an actual struggle for me not to try and take a bite, so much did the smell resembled Dot's mouth-watering canned sardines.

The back pounding continued. I spat up more water, and at last got something like a proper lungful of air, though I was still too weak—and bewildered—to move. I did manage a little *mrow*, though, as the Deep One (what else could it be?) carried me back to the blessed, blessed light.

"Spice!" Libby caterwauled, racing along the bank as I emerged from the tunnel. "Are you all right?"

I coughed in response, and got more solid whacks on the spine for it. I had to *mrow* again to make the thing stop.

The Deep One who carried me waded toward shore, passing close by his companion, the one who'd attacked Rob. That Deep One appeared to still be holding Rob underwater, though by now Rob's hands drifted lifelessly across the surface of the river, and his feet no longer kicked. I was pleased that the water was opaque enough not to reveal more of the corpse.

Without any further ado, the Deep One deposited me on the bank, a sodden, humbled mess of a cat. Shivering like mad, I limped around to face my savior.

This was the first good look I'd gotten at a Deep One, and I'm sorry to say they were just as ugly as I'd always presumed: their flat, noseless faces and dead-fish eyes combined the worst aspects of human and piscine features. It was hard to say whether they were more amphibian or fish-like, overall. The rubbery, slimy skin and generally fleshy surface of the Deep One was distinctly froggy, but the transparent fins that fluttered along his forearms, and the scattering of iridescent scales across his shoulders and back, fell more on the fish end of the scale.

This one blinked at me, his white eyelids meeting vertically across his staring yellow eyes, and opened his mouth wide, to emit strange gurgles. I was so fixated upon the mouthful of needle-sharp teeth, I paid no attention to the bizarre noises.

"Spice, are you ok?" Dot asked, slinking toward me, her wary eyes fixed upon the Deep One.

"It's *talking* to you, Spice," Libby remarked with awe.

I realized that it was, and with an effort concentrated on the guttural, gulping sounds, trying to discern the creature's meaning. Alas, it was no use. I couldn't make out a single word. I flattened my ears sadly and slowly blinked, trying to communicate back in feline fashion: "I'm sorry, I don't understand, but thank you."

The Deep One reached for me. I winced, but managed not to duck, as its slimy, webbed hand patted me on the head. Then it hooked a finger beneath my jaw and, very gently, scratched. It was just the right place for a cat, and I was shocked the creature somehow knew that. In my surprise, a little trickle of a purr emerged. The toothy, lipless mouth stretched in a grimace that might have been a smile.

The Deep One engaged in drowning Rob waded over to join us; it still clutched the occultist's now-floppy wrist, I noted, and was dragging the body with it beneath the waves. A third Deep One arose from the depths and joined them. They held a conference of some kind, while we cats retreated a little up the beach and held our own. It consisted mostly of the others licking me vigorously, and making smart remarks about how bad I tasted, and how stupid I looked with no tail.

We were all still in the vital process of grooming when the first Deep One lugged himself out of the river. Flat feet flapping upon the fungus-covered rock, he (it was now *obviously* a he) approached us. Though wary, we watched him kneel down upon the white, fluffy carpet, and open his webbed hand to display what rested in his fleshy, oozing palm.

What he held was a beautiful piece of gold-work, the loveliest I'd seen in any lifetime. It appeared to be a heavy bangle, shaped by the goldsmith's art into the delicate forms of coral, then carved with perfect renditions of tiny, scaled fish, and embedded with chips of an opalescent stone.

The Deep One gestured to me. I rose, and held my head high, as he fastened the bracelet around my neck. It fit perfectly, though I admit it was heavy. No insubstantial bit of plating, this—it had to be solid gold.

The Deep One ducked his head to me, and I dipped my head in return. This seemed to please him, and I was treated to another toothy grimace. Then he rose and flapped his way back to the river. A graceless, gruesome figure on land, once he dove back into the oily waters, he was nothing more than a sleek, fast-moving streak. His companions also ducked below the surface and jetted off, just swift shadows moving upriver, and soon gone from our view entirely.

Not so Rob. Abandoned by his killer, his body at last bobbed to the surface. It lay face-down, with the arms extended overhead, as if at any moment it might begin swimming once more. I admit I watched it for a long, nervous moment, somehow expecting that curly head to raise itself, dripping, from the water, and bare its teeth in that vicious smile.

But all the corpse did was began to drift, with agonizing slowness, toward the tunnel entrance. There it would join the corpse of Neil, who, if not dead now, surely would be soon; and there it might have joined my own pathetic, floating little body, had it not been for the Deep One's spontaneous act of kindness.

Shuddering at the thought, I fell to grooming my chest nervously. This ceased when Dot began nosing at the jewelry around my neck, examining it from all angles. "Pretty," she announced at last.

"Not as pretty as our new allies," I told her.

"Hmph. They would be *fish*," Libby sniffed disapprovingly, and sneezed. "So. Now what?"

We looked about ourselves. Empty cloaks lay scattered on the floor, surrounded by still-squirming piles of maggots—which, of course, we carefully avoided. Some little way distant, next to the stone altar, Cinnamon examined the remains of my tail. Head carried fiercely upright to support my majestic new collar, I shuffled toward her, to take a look for myself.

"You don't think" she said, as I approached, "that if we take it with us, the vet could put it back on?"

I sniffed dispiritedly at the sad plume of fur, lying bloodied on the white, hairy fungus. He really had cut off quite a lot—three-quarters of the length at least. Damn, but I was going to look ugly for the rest of this lifetime. "Forget it," I told her, with a sigh. "Look at it, in all that nasty stuff. It's probably contaminated. And what if a maggot crawled in?" I hissed at the very idea.

"We need to get out of here," Dot called toward us, already padding determinedly toward the cavern's back corner, where the shadowed entrance to the spiral staircase awaited. "The sooner, the better."

"All right," I said. Abruptly, I felt utterly exhausted; perhaps shock was setting in. "First, though, let's just…get away from these maggots, and…take a rest…"

"Can't," Cinnamon said sharply. "Listen."

Dutifully, I listened. Though the six night-gaunts still circled and looped above us, their noise did not obscure the distant, echoing flaps of many, many wings.

"They're coming back up the tunnel!" Libby exclaimed, pupils ballooning in size. "We have to get out of here, now! Now!"

I stared across the cavern, at the first stone steps of the long stairway, and what was left of my tail drooped. Even without the bracelet weighing me down, could I make it up those stairs quickly enough? Could I race past the things that lurked in the side passages, and climb past the secret door of the crypt, and dash through the red doors of the church? Could I then find someplace to hide in a Kingsport that was not my own, someplace that would conceal me for hours as I awaited the salvation of dawn? Not if the cloaked ones were mounted on fast-flying night-gaunts, I couldn't.

"We'll never make it," said Dot, coming to precisely the same conclusion I had, at precisely the same moment. "We'll have to hide."

"Don't be daft!" Libby shrilled. "They'll search the whole place, when they see what's happened here! And close all the doors, too!"

Cinnamon coughed. We ignored her. She coughed again, this time in a clear pay-attention-to-me way.

"What, Cinnamon?" I snapped.

"I have an idea," she said. "I have…a memory. But I don't know, for sure…"

"Stars' sake, girl," I told her, "if you have an idea, try it!" The flapping had grown nearer, I could tell, but it was becoming difficult to hear over the ringing in my ears. Forget climbing that winding staircase—I'd be lucky not to faint right here.

Cinnamon dropped the key talisman—which, incredibly, she'd been carrying this entire time—at my feet. Leaping upon the altar, she stared upwards, at the night-gaunts who drifted aimlessly overhead.

Then she *gibbered.*

It was a sound I'd never heard a cat make, and my hair all stood on end. Libby's pupils flared larger, which I wouldn't have thought possible, and Dot hissed, her already-ugly face squashed into a hideous grimace.

Yet the results were immediate. First one night-gaunt circled down to a landing, then another. They craned their blank, featureless faces toward Cinnamon, who *gibbered* at them again.

In a cacophony of wing-beats, the returning night-gaunts burst forth from the tunnel, a flock of enormous bats straight from the depths of hell. At the same time, the two night-gaunts in front of Cinnamon pumped their wings and rose into the air. The first one picked up Cinnamon, grasping her around the middle with its long fingers, and then flew straight at me. I knew what it intended.

With what courage I had left, I crouched down and picked up the talisman—and I didn't run. I did, however, close my eyes as those long fingers wrapped themselves around my abdomen, squeezing my ribs and tickling me with the tips of terrifying talons. The night-gaunt flapped, and the earth dropped away. I bit down on the talisman so as not to howl. My eyes were still tight-shut, so I couldn't see what was happening, but my stomach was floating somewhere around my throat, and my heart stuttered with every swoop.

At last I could stand it no longer. I opened my eyes—just as the night-gaunt dove for the narrow entrance of the stairwell. Once again I bit down on the iron key in terror, certain I was about to be dashed against the rock. Yet in the space of a heartbeat, the huge creature somehow fit itself neatly through the entrance, like threading a deadly needle, and beat its way upwards. For a few moments, the stairs were nothing but a blur, less than half a tail-length from my dangling paws. One dip, one slip, and I'd break my foot upon the unforgiving stone. Then, the light from the cavern was gone. We were flying in total darkness, under exactly the same conditions—except that now, of course, I couldn't see a thing. I closed my eyes again, and I think I must have fainted, because when I opened them once more, we were soaring far, far above the earth.

My heart nearly stopped with fear, as I observed the black waves pounding the white sand far below my paws. Yet nothing altered after long moments of anxious, shuddery breathing: the night-gaunt's ticklish fingers never shifted, nor did it duck or dip as it had in the caverns.

Eventually, I relaxed very, very slightly. Drifting through the cloudless, starry skies, sniffing the fresh, salty air of the ocean—these were good, wholesome things indeed, after all that had occurred below.

At last I craned my head to look at Cinnamon, held securely in the night-gaunt's other paw. "How did you do that?" I asked frankly. "How did you *know*?"

She hesitated, looking at me sideways through slitted eyes. "Don't tell the others?"

I purred in assent, though it took an effort, for the night-gaunt's tight grip squeezed me.

She looked away, out upon the ocean. "I *think*...I'm beginning to remember...that I wasn't always a cat."

My ears twitched in surprise, but there was no time to inquire further. A second night-gaunt had just soared upwards from the white spire of the church below. Our night-gaunt drifted in its direction, and the two began to circle one another other, high above the town. In the second night-gaunt's grasp were Dot and Libby, who dangled limply from its long-fingered, monkey-like paws. I was irrationally pleased that both looked as profoundly uncomfortable as I felt.

"Now what?" Dot called, once they were close enough.

"We're still not home!" Libby complained.

I looked. Indeed, we weren't. The roofs below sported antiquated shingles, and there was not a single street-lamp in sight. Indeed, there was not a single light in the town. All the lit windows had been extinguished, and all the lanterns were, apparently, still well below ground.

What was this place? I wondered. Was it really just the Kingsport of the past? That might explain the aged houses, perhaps, but not the lack of footprints, or of sound, or of any life beyond that awful parody of humanity, disguised in cloaks and wax masks. Was this some other realm altogether? Or was it a sort of splinter off the material world, neither its own dimension, nor quite fully ours? And if so, had it been discovered, or created? And if created, then for what purpose? I would have plenty of questions for Solar, the next time I encountered the former wizard's familiar—but this reminded me that I hadn't yet answered Dot.

"I don't know," I admitted. "Do you think they saw us leave?"

Light blossomed below, startling us all. It poured from the windows of the church, casting great yellow patches onto the glittering snow. Once again, I heard the *flap-flap* of many night-gaunts' wings, and was not unduly surprised when one of the devilish beasts soared from between the great red doors, carrying on its back a cloaked rider, who bore in turn a golden lantern. Another followed, and another, and another. The great black silhouettes spiraled higher into the moonless sky, coming ever nearer. Mere darkness would not conceal us for long.

"Yeah," said Dot grimly. "I'm pretty sure they did."

At that moment, by the grace of the great stars whose fiery deaths birthed our world, I was struck by heavenly inspiration.

"Get this thing to fly over the town," I ordered Cinnamon.

Cinnamon blinked at me, clearly taken aback.

"It's my turn to save the day," I said.

She made that peculiar, unfeline sound again, and our night-gaunt dove forward, causing my stomach to surge as well as reigniting my terror—despite knowing better, my paws flailed and my claws unsheathed, irrationally seeking traction in empty space. The second night-gaunt, carrying Dot and Libby, fell in behind us.

In the corner of my eye, I saw a pursuing night-gaunt alter its wheeling, searching course, and glide smoothly toward us. We'd been spotted. A second swooped in our direction, then a third, then a fourth. Caught in the night-gaunt's grasp, I couldn't look behind me, but I could hear the wings of our pursuers beating closer and closer, faceless monsters bearing their faceless masters upon their backs. How many were behind us now? Time for me to make good on my word, and save the day, indeed.

The talisman still clicked between my teeth: it was pure good fortune that it hadn't slipped from my mouth during my semi-faint. As we soared over the town, as the flapping of our pursuers swelled to an uproar, I bit the disgusting, urine-soaked charm tighter, and focused.

Open the door.

Then I prayed, to any god or saint or spirit that would listen, that the talisman was truly so simple to use. I'd thought it must be easy, when I'd seen Cinnamon open the path to the island; since then, though, I'd had to drastically revise my opinion on the subject of Cinnamon's intelligence. I could only hope that I'd been more accurate in my assessment of the key.

A slit appeared in the air just ahead of us, a thin band of different-colored sky: not clear and dark like the sky of Old

Kingsport, but cloudy with snow and glowing with the light pollution of a thoroughly modern town.

I'd done it!

At the last moment, I wondered whether our night-gaunts might try to avoid the narrow corridor through reality, seeing it as an obstacle rather than an entrance. However, either the night-gaunt was too stupid to think much about it, or it was clever enough to perceive an opportunity. Either way, in the mere twitch of a tail, we'd soared through the talisman's door—and, unbelievably, we were flying over Kingsport. *Our* Kingsport.

Street-lamps marked out the wide, paved roads that criss-crossed below. Heavy clouds tossed the city's light back upon itself, surrounding us in a soft, warm glow nearly as bright as the missing moonlight. There were multi-colored Christmas lights pegged to the roofs, and the red brake lights of cars, and the sounds of honking and people and stupid barking dogs. We were home.

With a great effort, I twisted round, and finally managed to sneak a peek over my shoulder. I saw no gap in the sky behind us, and no hideous wings beat the air save for those that carried us. Whether the door had sealed itself against the cloaked ones, or they had simply refrained from pursuing us further, would remain forever unclear. I couldn't give a damn.

We were home.

I heaved a sigh of profound relief—and the key slipped from between my teeth. It fell, a rapidly diminishing black speck, to the earth far below. Disoriented from the flight, I could identify no landmarks, and thus had no idea where it might have landed.

To hell with it, I thought, and sighed again. We were home.

13

Mortal

It was the witching hour, which all real witches know is the darkest time before the dawn. The night-gaunts deposited us in an empty lot just outside the city, near the new housing development. There they were dismissed by Cinnamon, to return to their rightful home in the dreamlands. One moment, the four-winged, faceless creatures were as real and solid as we; the next, they were gone, we knew not where. I doubted any of us particularly cared.

Good-byes were exchanged in the form of long cheek swipes and short grooming sessions; I believe we were still confirming that we'd all emerged alive. I know I was astonished to discover that such was the case. At last assured of our continued mortal existence, we finally went our separate ways, and wended our solitary paths, as all good cats ought to. Slipping behind towering snow-drifts, and avoiding the overbright street lights, I finally turned my nose toward home.

Bug the kitten had promised daylight would dissipate the Dark Yule; that night I discovered she'd been wrong. Long before the first ray of dawn, when I looked to See That Which

Cannot Be Seen, I could perceive no shadows, no spirits, no ghosts, no time-slips, no fluttering fragments of the past, and certainly—thank the stars—no more night-gaunts. Morwen might hope for a happy Christmas yet.

Of course, there were other kinds of encounters to be had: this was Kingsport, after all. I hissed at the vampire from Burying Hill as she drifted past, her cheeks rosy with some unlucky soul's life-force; she snickered at me, but moved on anyway. Near a patch of trees I caught a whiff of something charnel, and wondered whether the ghouls weren't already returning to their extensive network of tunnels. But this was all quite normal and expected, for a cat upon her nightly rounds. If anything unusual was out that night, it was me: tailless, half-drowned, stumbling with exhaustion, and bearing a golden collar fit for a fairytale feline queen.

I admit that I was beyond weary when I approached our old, rickety farmhouse. I almost went around the back, to use the cat flap, but belatedly remembered that it had been nailed shut. I'd probably have to paw at the front door and cry until Morwen came to let me in, and wouldn't she be in a mood *then*. Moping, the gold bracelet sitting heavy upon me, I dragged myself up the snow-laden steps of the porch.

The door slammed open, making me startle. I froze, fully prepared to flee, but all that emerged from the house was Morwen, wrapped in Her Husband's ancient brown robe and wearing his down-at-heel moccasins.

Pumpkin Spice! she exclaimed. With an effort she bent down and picked me up. I purred feebly as she carried me over to the porch swing and, heedless of the dusting of snow, sat down heavily upon it.

Spice, you had me so worried. What happened? And then—*Your tail!*

I sighed and let my head fall to her lap, mewing pitifully at her. She rubbed my jaw and my back and every bit of me that she could reach. In response, I closed my eyes and purred like I meant it.

What's this? I understood her to say. Her fingers plucked at the bracelet around my neck, until the exquisite piece unhinged and came away in her hand. I shook my ruff with some relief—it *had* been heavy—and opened my eyes just a slit, to enjoy her astonished expression. *Spice, where did you get this?*

"From the Deep Ones," I told her, knowing she wouldn't understand. "The Deep Ones presented it to me, for defeating the mad, maggoty wizards, and preventing them from escaping their timeless prison." I wasn't really sure about the 'timeless prison' part, but it sounded good. And besides, she didn't—

Deep Ones?

I opened my eyes fully, and stared directly into hers.

Had she understood me?

Morwen glanced back at the bracelet, and frowned. Setting it aside, she turned her attention to what was left of my tail. I winced, but continued bravely to purr, as she very gently touched the bloodied stump.

Hold still, Pumpkin Spice.

I closed my eyes once more and submitted to her ministrations. Quietly, Morwen murmured—a spell, a prayer, a shopping list, I couldn't say. The area around my tail began to warm, and to tingle in a pins-and-needles fashion. At first it was pleasant, and then it became uncomfortable. At last it was actively painful, and my purr deepened into an unhappy growl, which ended on a lengthy warning hiss. Damn it, what *was* she doing back there?

Morwen lifted her hand, with murmured apologies, and at once I twisted around to look at my tail. The fur was still bloody, but the tip of my mauled appendage bore a fresh, ugly scab—a scab it shouldn't have formed for a half-day or more to come.

Contrite, I licked Morwen's hand, and emitted the loudest purr I'd ever managed. Morwen smiled and scratched my chin, in just the same place as the Deep One.

Things are going to be different now, Spice, she said. I could hear the suppressed excitement bubbling under her words. *You'll see.*

Tucking the bracelet deep into the pocket of her robe, she picked me up and carried me inside, up the carpeted stairs, where I was permitted to check on my sleeping baby…

…before Morwen gave me a bath.

14

From the Author

I hope you enjoyed *The Dark Yule*, the first installment in the Pumpkin Spice Tales. If you did, and you have a minute to spare, please leave a review—customer reviews are the single best way for any book to find new readers. Your help is very much appreciated!

If you'd like to learn more about the Pumpkin Spice Tales, the other stories of New Kingsport, or the loathsome, twisted minds that created them, you can read more (if you dare) at flockhall.com. Sign up there to become a member of the Flock and get access to free bonus scenes, character interviews, book-related art, discounts, giveaways, ~~leeches~~ and more.

Have an unspeakable day!

15

The Dead Witch

Check out the first chapter of Book Two, The Dead Witch, *available now on Amazon.*

Chapter 1: Obsidian

In a distant land of dream, at the center of a crumbling temple, was a black pool of divination. I'd brought an offering to the pool and to the unseen spirits who guarded it: a fat, juicy, headless mouse. It was the last of many such little presents, for I owed these forgotten gods a great debt.

Carefully I nosed the mouse over the edge, and let it fall into the sacred pool with a muffled little *plop.* The tiny body floated for a moment, spinning slowly in the still waters, before slipping below the surface. I could see its silhouette drifting down, down, down. Then it was gone, and nothing disturbed the pool's obsidian depths.

The pool was surrounded by a wide, tiled ledge; the broken tiles, perhaps once blue, were now as gray as the clouds visible through the temple's shattered roof. Curiously enough, the black waters of the pool did not reflect the gloomy sky above. They remained ebony, save for the occasional faint twinkle far below, come and gone so fast you could hardly swear you'd seen it.

I sat on the ledge in proper meditative fashion: paws together, with my lovely plumed tail curled around them, and my eyes fixed upon my own reflection, which blinked back at me with uncanny clarity.

"Spirits of the temple and of prophecy," I said. "I command you, by the One and the Many, and by the barbarous names of old. By the gods and the spirits of the worlds of dream and of being, by the white light and the red, I conjure you to obey me. Nor will you find my words without value, my promises unkept, or my offerings unworthy of your great and particular powers—as you should know by now."

My tail twitched, betraying my nerves, as I uttered my well-rehearsed question: "What will happen when Morwen's new baby is born? And how can I best help her at that time?"

A loud wail echoed through the temple. The hair shot up all along my spine. I braced myself upon the ledge, back arched, claws extended, ready to flee or to fight as required. Almost in the same moment, however, the less instinctual part of my mind reconsidered. Surely the cry of a healthy baby was a good sign?

The wail repeated itself, and I hissed at the sound, which shivered right through me. That was no baby. That was the sound of a woman in terrible pain.

My ears flattened against my head, and my tail thrashed against the stone. Nonetheless I leaned forward to study the waters, which were no longer glassy, but choppy and rough, as if responding to unseen currents below. Shadows and light gleamed here and there upon the broken surface, but they had not yet cohered into a clear vision.

There! A face was forming in the ripples. A stark white face, with its lower jaw thrust forward, and its bottom teeth jutting above its blackened lip. Was it a muzzle? Could it be an animal? No, for the upper portion was too flat, and a few strings of human hair still clung to the rubbery scalp. The eyes that glared at me were a watery pink...

"Bloody hell," I spat. "That damn ghoul *again?*"

My own reflection became clearer in the water as well, and the ghoul's face loomed just above it. It appeared, to all intents and purposes, that the creature was standing behind me. But when? And where? There was no hint in the vision as to how this might occur.

Just as I bent to examine the water more closely, my whiskers quivered in a sudden movement of air. My tail brushed something warm, something that was not stone. Legs bunching beneath me, I leaped vigorously aside.

The ghoul standing behind me missed me by a hair.

He whirled at once, crooked teeth bared, and lunged again. My foot slipped on the slick tiles, and I could not jump away in time. His clawed hands clamped upon me, slamming me to the floor. I yowled with fury and scratched every inch of him I could reach, but those terrible talons just crunched down harder and harder, until I shrieked with the cracking of my bones.

Panting, I trembled, helpless, in the albino ghoul's grasp. He stuck his terrible face down next to mine, forcing me to breathe his carrion breath, and to stare at the white, protruding fangs a paws-breadth from my face.

"No Deep One to save you now, kitty cat," the ghoul blubbered at me. A long string of drool stretched from his blackened lip, hovering just above my nose. I twisted but could not escape its approach. "No other kitty friends. You're *mine*."

"Idiot!" I said, panting all the while—I could hardly squeeze air into my lungs, and each breath sent stabbing pains racing along my ribs. I was in very bad shape. "You know I'm mortal! All I have to do is wake up!"

The ghoul grinned at me, a ghastly sight. There was something red caught between his teeth. "So wake up," he suggested, with an air of innocence.

Yes, if only I could wake up, I would be quite safe. I knew that, and yet—and yet—I couldn't. No matter how I blinked and twitched and begged the stars internally, I couldn't wake up.

What happened to a dreamer who died in the dreamlands? I wasn't sure. I never had.

The ghoul sneered at my distress. Arching his head back, he opened his mouth wide, wide, wider, until I could see nothing of him but that awful, gaping red mouth, and the double row of sharp teeth within, designed to crunch even the heartiest bones.

The teeth descended. I closed my eyes—and felt a sharp pain in my tail. It shouldn't have competed with the black talons buried within the muscle of my shoulder, or the broken ribs pricking along my lungs, or the first scrape of teeth as the mouth closed over my head. But it did, because it was real.

I seized the sensation and followed it, blocking out all else, allowing the pain to pull me upwards, to the very surface of sleep. Trembling upon the verge of consciousness, I with an effort opened my eyes—my *real* eyes—and blinked into the bright light streaming from the window.

Thank the stars. I was awake.

My baby still had a good grip on my tail—or, rather, the stubby remains of my once beautiful tail, which had been cut off by a truly unspeakable creature only three months before. The little human boy looked at me, looked at his own chubby hand, and gave the stump a second good yank. I blinked lovingly at him and tapped his sticky fingers with my paw, claws well-sheathed. This did absolutely nothing to deter my baby and he naturally pulled a third time, harder than before.

That did it for me. I was grateful for his unconscious aid, but I wasn't *that* grateful. Rolling to my feet, I swept my tail out of his grasp and stalked away, head high to compensate for the lack of a sassily waving plume. Oh, well. At least I still had a tail when I dreamed.

And speaking of dreams, I had to find some way to tell Morwen what I'd seen—and heard—in the temple. Since she didn't speak cat, and I didn't speak human, that would be far from easy.

The kettle was whistling in the kitchen, and Her Husband was lifting it off the stove. I slunk past him, belly low to the linoleum. Her Husband and I never got along at the best of times, and he'd been particularly nervy of late. I thought I knew why, too. It wasn't only because his wife was about to deliver their second child.

Rather than engage with Her Husband, I skittered up the shabby, carpeted stairs to the bedrooms. A reek of paint hung in the air, and a bucket and brush had been abandoned at the third bedroom's door. That bedroom had heretofore been a dusty space reserved for guests; now it was to be a second nursery for this newest human addition. That is, assuming the birth went well…

I poked my head inside the nursery-to-be, which was barren of furniture save for a lone rocking chair. Morwen wasn't in there. But I did spot something new hanging in the window, something that swayed and twisted in the light.

I blinked and altered my vision in that special, feline way, to see That Which Cannot Be Seen. Upon second sight, I was scarcely surprised that the object in the window gleamed faintly, with a curious little twinkle that indicated magic.

I padded over to the window. The object appeared to be a cross made from rough-cut twigs, wound about with blue thread in a distinctive, web-like pattern. The shine of magic upon it was discernible, but very faint indeed—hardly more than a suggestion. Dangling from a long string, the little charm looked downright tantalizing; I stretched upwards against the wall, as high as I could, and batted in its general direction. However Morwen, who was no fool (at least when it came to felines), had hung the talisman well beyond my reach. Disappointed, I turned away from the charm with a long, bitter *maaoooow*, and continued my search for the temptress who'd designed it.

Since she'd abandoned her work in the nursery, it wasn't hard to guess where she might be. I dashed up the next staircase, a bare wooden thing that creaked alarmingly. The door to the attic was slightly open, enabling me to squeeze inside.

In the middle of the chalk circle, with her black skirts spread around her, sat Morwen. Her pregnant belly was simply enormous at this point; it rested between her thighs as she bent over her finicky work. A stick of sandalwood incense burned a tail's-length from her thigh, and the floor was cluttered with the tools of her practice: a knife, yarn, stubs of half-burned candles, a bowl of salt, a bottle of whiskey, and the iridescent feather of a magpie.

With a *mrrow!* of greeting I stepped cautiously over the boundaries of the circle, careful not to smudge the laboriously-drawn signs of the elements that bordered her working space. Morwen extended her hand at my approach, and after a salutary sniff of her fingers, I grazed my jaw along their tips, scratching the itchy place that exists under the chin of every cat.

Look, Spice, Morwen said. I couldn't actually understand her babbling vocalizations, no more than I could understand the birds that sang and squawked in our bushes. Because of our connection, however, I could grasp the meaning behind her words. *Look at this. It's a spirit trap.*

She dangled her work in front of me—an exact copy of the little charm in the nursery window, only this one was green instead of blue. My pupils dilated as it twisted on its string. The threads gleamed in my enhanced sight as I crouched low, my stubby tail quivering.

No! Morwen told me sternly, but it was too late. I'd already sprung up, both paws extended, claws fully unsheathed to seize the delightful toy. I got it! I yanked it from Morwen's grasp and pounced upon it, bearing the talisman down to the floor. It was mine! The beast was mine!

No, Spice, no! Bad cat! Morwen scolded, as I rolled onto my back, kicking the loosening green threads with both back paws. Disembowel the creature! Kill it! Kill it!

Goddamnit, cat, Morwen grumbled, and snatched it out of my paws. I let her take it—I'd had my fun. Patiently I waited, tail still twitching with excitement, while she mumbled and grouched and rewound the threads I'd pulled free.

"A spirit trap, huh?" I said, when I guessed her temper had

cooled somewhat. "Interesting color choice. I would've gone with red, myself. Spirits are drawn to red."

Morwen ignored my sally and continued winding the threads. I sighed internally. There had been a few brief, shining moments of true communication between us three months ago, during the events of the Dark Yule. Morwen had actually understood what I was saying to her, even comprehending such specifics as "Let me out!" and "Deep Ones!" That was also when Morwen had successfully worked magic upon my tail, inducing a hearty, healing scab days before one could be expected to form. We'd both been thrilled, I think; we'd believed that our lives had changed forever.

We'd thought wrong. Or, rather, *I* was coming to the conclusion that we'd thought wrong. Morwen had awoken the next morning with all of her pre-marital interest in witchcraft revived. She'd pulled down all her magic books, and returned from the grocery store laden with spices and herbs. A dozen little charms were now scattered around the house, and heaven forbid Her Husband or my baby even glance at one wrong, let alone touch it. So all-consuming had her passion become that the baby's room still wasn't ready—because whenever Morwen swore that she was going to finish the nursery, she snuck off to the attic instead.

And what was the result of this feverish activity and study? Very little, so far as I could tell. True, her charms got a bit better each time, but they were far from the most effective wards. In magical terms, they were a four-foot chain-link fence, as opposed to a twelve-foot high brick wall: more of a suggestion than a genuine deterrent. That suggestion was enough for any of your garden-variety spirits, but Kingsport had more than its fair share of darker entities.

Such as the ghouls, for example, who'd been in Kingsport since the first body was first laid to rest on Burying Hill, and whose long-lasting wrath seemed fixated upon me.

But the magic didn't concern me as much: I had to assume that Morwen would eventually either learn better, or give up. What truly worried me was our inability to communicate. I'd attempted repeatedly since the Dark Yule to get Morwen to hear me, and had failed every time. She would try to listen, I could tell, and she had become more attentive and observant, but the gap still stretched far between us. Genuine understanding remained out of reach.

And yet, somehow, I had to convey to Morwen what I'd heard in the dreamlands temple, before my vision had been so violently interrupted. Even the memory of that high-pitched wail of pain sent tingles down my spine, trembling each hair upright.

Morwen finished her work and set it aside. She reached for a black-handled knife, doubtless preparing to consecrate the charm. I intervened, interposing myself between her and the blade.

Move, Spice! Morwen commanded. I reacted the way any proper cat would. I sat on the knife, and glared at her.

Ugh, Spice... Morwen rubbed her belly and heaved a sigh, doubtless feeling quite sorry for herself. I knew she'd be feeling even sorrier shortly, and so persisted in my attempts. Getting off the knife, I meowed plaintively, and butted my head into her belly.

Ooph, Spice, don't.

Sitting determinedly in front of her, I gently patted her stomach with a velvety paw, then stared her straight in the eye. She frowned at me.

What is it, Spice?

Encouraged, I patted her belly again, and continued to fix my gaze upon her. Her frown deepened with concentration.

Is something wrong with the baby?

Morwen sounded distressed—but at least I'd aroused her concern. I patted the belly a final time, then placed both paws upon her stomach and reared up, to touch my nose to hers.

Ow, Spice!

I got off her and stared at her, tail twitching, trying to gauge the impact of my efforts. Morwen certainly appeared troubled. She pulled up her shirt and examined her belly, which to my mind looked ready to burst. Human pregnancies astounded me. All that time and discomfort, for just one baby—maybe two at the most? Highly inefficient, not to mention extraordinarily difficult for the females.

Not for the first time, I blessed the stars for incarnating me repeatedly as a cat. Every lifetime I could remember, I'd been a cat—and I intended to keep it that way, thank you very much.

Maybe I'd better go into the clinic, Morwen said. I *mrrow*ed in affirmation, and rose to get out of her way.

Or... she went on. *Hmm.*

There was a stack of books to her left; she pulled out one and opened it, resting it atop her stomach to read. I suppose it was a grimoire, of sorts, though what self-respecting grimoire was covered with a colorful cartoon of a grinning witch perched saucily on a broomstick, I couldn't say.

Several long minutes passed, while Morwen silently flipped through the book. At last I got bored and wandered off to a corner, where I discovered interesting evidence of new mouse activity: three tiny feces, all relatively fresh. It was spring now, after all, if just barely. The equinox was approaching, and the deadlock of snow and ice was beginning to lift. Wild mice would begin breeding again, and seeking new nests for themselves and their offspring. I would have to be vigilant in the coming days and weeks.

My ear swiveled at the sound of Morwen's voice, and glanced over my shoulder, to see her dipping a length of blue string in a jar of water. Curious, I ambled back toward the circle, and sat at its edge, my paw at the tip of the symbol for Fire.

Morwen spit upon the string, leaving a gooey glob dangling from the middle, then ran it through her fingers to spread the saliva along its length. This accomplished, she waved the string through the smoke, muttering indecipherable words as she did so.

Now, what should I say? Morwen murmured. *Power...hour... what rhymes with peace?*

At last she came to some conclusion, for she nodded briskly, cleared her throat, and sat more fully upright. As her nimble fingers knotted the bottom of the string, she softly chanted an incantation, which I understood to mean something like this:

Here I bind full labor power
Until my baby's birthing hour.
The knot's undone, my power's unleashed.
My baby slides out like she's greased
And we're both safe and full at peace.

This incantation she repeated for six further knots. When it was finished, she opened a box nearby and selected an old, black scarf, one I recognized from her college days. I recalled rolling myself into its silken folds as a wee kitten, and chewing the tassels at the end. In this fine old scarf Morwen tucked the string.

Now she stood—a lengthy and, judging by the sounds she

made, excruciating process. Waddling over to her desk, she pulled out a small drawer and rested the little black packet inside, before closing it firmly.

I'll finish charging it later, she said, more to herself than to me, I'm sure. I meowed at her, catching her attention once more. She smiled and wiggled her fingers, but didn't bend to pet me, which was probably for the best in her top-heavy state.

Don't worry, Spice. I'll still go to the doc.

Her Husband was calling up the stairs. I never could understand Her Husband properly—very little sympathy existed between him and me—but judging by the exasperation in his tone, Morwen's tea had gotten cold…again.

I followed Morwen to the door, but as she began her precarious walk down the stairs, I stopped to stare over my shoulder at the desk. Surely I should've felt pleased—by combining magic with medical advice, Morwen was addressing any potential problem at every level she could. And yet…something about that little charm unsettled me.

Get the The Dead Witch *on Amazon now, in ebook or paperback format.*

About the Author

R.M. Callahan is an author and narrative designer who is frankly glad she can't See That Which Cannot Be Seen. She currently lives in the Land of Blue Dragon (Vietnam) with her husband M.R. Callahan, two rascally children, two equally mischievous dogs, and a brown cat that bears no resemblance to Pumpkin Spice whatsoever.

The Callahans together write the Tales of New Kingsport, a set of intertwined series that are full of Mythos-influenced mayhem. They also run the Callahan Creatives Agency and have written for a wide variety of games and related content.

You can connect with me on:
- https://www.flockhall.com
- https://www.facebook.com/rmcallahanbooks

Subscribe to my newsletter:
- https://www.flockhall.com/contact

Also by R.M. Callahan

R.M. and M.R. Callahan together write the Tales of New Kingsport, a set of intertwined series full of Mythos-influenced mayhem. See all their books at www.flockhall.com.

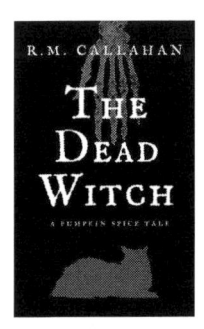

The Dead Witch
Pumpkin Spice—Maine Coon cat and part-time familiar—refuses to let her witch die. But Morwen's birth spell has gone seriously wrong, and now Spice has hours (or less) to break the enchantment before it kills both mother and child.

Which is the perfect time for Spice to learn a terrible secret: The Dark Yule is far from finished with her.

On that dreadful night, Spice accidentally let someone escape. Someone whose very presence has awakened another creature.

A creature long-hidden and forgotten, in a realm neither here nor there, but desperately clawing its way towards our world…

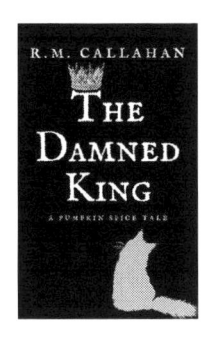

The Damned King

Spice loves her witch…but not the creature possessing her.

Pumpkin Spice, Maine Coon cat and part-time familiar, *knew* Morwen's magical mentors were bad news. But did Morwen listen to Spice's sage advice? Hell no! So instead, Spice has to beg her frenemy, the ghoul-king, to drive Morwen's tormentors out of town.

But those wicked witches have friends in low places…

Printed in Great Britain
by Amazon